DISEASES & DISORDERS

618.7
MIL

Postpartum Depression

Titles in the Diseases and Disorders series include:

Acne
AIDS
Alzheimer's Disease
Anorexia and Bulimia
Anthrax
Arthritis
Asthma
Attention Deficit Disorder
Autism
Bipolar Disorder
Birth Defects
Breast Cancer
Cerebral Palsy
Chronic Fatigue Syndrome
Cystic Fibrosis
Deafness
Diabetes
Down Syndrome
Dyslexia
Epilepsy
Fetal Alcohol Syndrome
Food Poisoning
Growth Disorders
Headaches
Heart Disease
Hemophilia
Hepatitis
Human Papillomavirus (HPV)
Leukemia
Lou Gehrig's Disease
Lyme Disease
Mad Cow Disease
Malaria
Malnutrition
Measles and Rubella
Meningitis
Mental Retardation
Multiple Sclerosis
Obesity
Ovarian Cancer
Parkinson's Disease
Phobias
SARS
Schizophrenia
Sexually Transmitted
    Diseases
Sleep Disorders
Smallpox
Strokes
Teen Depression
Toxic Shock Syndrome
Tuberculosis
West Nile Virus

DISEASES & DISORDERS

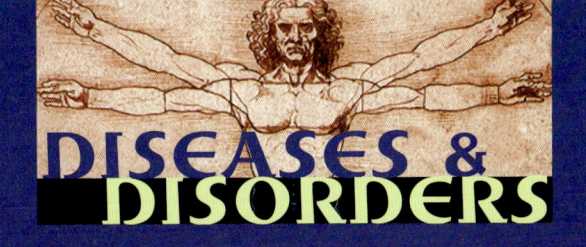

Postpartum Depression

Debra A. Miller

LUCENT BOOKS
A part of Gale, Cengage Learning

GALE
CENGAGE Learning

Detroit • New York • San Francisco • New Haven, Conn • Waterville, Maine • London

GALE
CENGAGE Learning™

© 2008 Gale, a part of Cengage Learning

For more information, contact
Lucent Books
27500 Drake Rd.
Farmington Hills, MI 48331-3535
Or you can visit our Internet site at gale.cengage.com

ALL RIGHTS RESERVED.
No part of this work covered by the copyright hereon may be reproduced or used in any form or by any means—graphic, electronic, or mechanical, including photocopying, recording, taping, Web distribution or information storage retrieval systems—without the written permission of the publisher.

Every effort has been made to trace the owners of copyrighted material.

LIBRARY OF CONGRESS CATALOGING-IN-PUBLICATION DATA

Miller, Debra A.
  Postpartum depression / by Debra A. Miller.
    p. cm. — (Diseases and disorders)
  Includes bibliographical references and index.
  ISBN-13: 978-1-4205-0001-1 (hardcover)
  1. Postpartum depression—Juvenile literature. I. Title.
  RG852.M55 2008
  618.7'6—dc22
                                                              2007032094

ISBN-10: 1-4205-0001-5

Printed in the United States of America
2 3 4 5 6 7 12 11 10 09 08

Table of Contents

Foreword   6

Introduction
   When Motherhood Becomes a Nightmare   8

Chapter 1
   What Is Postpartum Depression?   14

Chapter 2
   Diagnosis and Drug Treatment   30

Chapter 3
   Nondrug Therapies   44

Chapter 4
   Effects of PPD on the Child and Others   60

Chapter 5
   The Road to Recovery   72

Notes   84
Glossary   88
Organizations to Contact   94
For More Information   96
Index   99
Picture Credits   104
About the Author   104

FOREWORD

"The Most Difficult Puzzles Ever Devised"

Charles Best, one of the pioneers in the search for a cure for diabetes, once explained what intrigued him so about medical research: "It's not just the gratification of knowing one is helping people," he confided, "although that probably is a more heroic and selfless motivation. Those feelings may enter in, but truly, what I find best is the feeling of going toe to toe with nature, of trying to solve the most difficult puzzles ever devised. The answers are there somewhere, those keys that will solve the puzzle and make the patient well. But how will those keys be found?"

Since the dawn of civilization, nothing has so puzzled people—and often frightened them, as well—as the onset of illness in a body or mind that seemed healthy before. Being unable to reverse conditions such as a seizure, the inability of a heart to pump, or the sudden deterioration of muscle tone in a small child, or even to understand why they occur was unspeakably frustrating to healers. Even before there were names for such conditions, before they were understood at all, each was

Foreword

a reminder of how complex the human body was and how vulnerable.

While our grappling with understanding diseases has been frustrating at times, it has also provided some of humankind's most heroic accomplishments. Alexander Fleming's accidental discovery in 1928 of a mold that could be turned into penicillin has resulted in the saving of untold millions of lives. The isolation of the enzyme insulin has reversed what was once a death sentence for anyone with diabetes. There also have been great strides in combating conditions for which there is not yet a cure. Medicines can help AIDS patients live longer, diagnostic tools such as mammography and ultrasounds can help doctors find tumors while they are treatable, and laser surgery techniques have made the most intricate, minute operations routine.

This "toe-to-toe" competition with diseases and disorders is even more remarkable when viewed in a historical continuum. An astonishing amount of progress has been made in a very short time. Just two hundred years ago, the existence of germs as a cause of some diseases was unknown. In fact, less than 150 years ago a British surgeon named Joseph Lister had difficulty persuading his fellow doctors that washing their hands before delivering a baby might increase the chances of a healthy delivery (especially if they had just attended to a diseased patient)!

Each book in Lucent's Diseases and Disorders series explores a disease or disorder and the knowledge that has been accumulated (or discarded) by doctors through the years. Each book also examines the tools used for pinpointing a diagnosis, as well as the various means that are used to treat or cure a disease. Finally, new ideas are presented—techniques or medicines that may be on the horizon.

Frustration and disappointment are still part of medicine because not every disease or condition can be cured or prevented. But the limitations of knowledge are constantly being pushed outward; the "most difficult puzzles ever devised" are finding challengers every day.

INTRODUCTION

When Motherhood Becomes a Nightmare

Pregnancy and childbirth are supposed to be the best time of a woman's life, but the reality is often far from this ideal. As Diana Lynn Barnes, a clinical psychologist in Woodland Hills, California, explains, "We are told that pregnancy and childbirth should be the happiest time of your life, but that's a cultural myth. . . . It's a very tumultuous time in the life of a woman, and one of the most stressful periods in her life."[1] In fact, during the period following pregnancy and childbirth, called "postpartum," a significant number of women experience varying levels of depression—from relatively mild feelings of sadness and fatigue to full-blown mental illness. In some of the most serious cases of postpartum depression (PPD), the disorder has even led some mothers to kill their own children or themselves.

Worst Possible Outcome

One of the most publicized recent cases of PPD-related homicide was that of Andrea Yates, a 36-year-old mother from Houston, Texas, who killed all five of her children: Noah (7), John (5), Paul (3), Luke (2), and Mary (6 months). Yates had a history of serious postpartum depression, beginning in July 1999 with the birth of her fourth child, Luke. After being hospitalized for trying to commit suicide, Yates was prescribed an antidepressant medication and released, but she failed to

When Motherhood Becomes a Nightmare

take her medication and continued to deteriorate. She began having hallucinations and refused to feed her children, believing they were eating too much. Finally, Yates was hospitalized again and successfully treated with various medications, including powerful antipsychotic drugs. At the time, her doctor warned her that having more babies would likely lead to a recurrence of psychotic behaviors.

Yates ignored the doctor's warning, however, and conceived a fifth child, Mary, who was born on November 30, 2000. Yates did well for awhile, but in March 2001, her father died, and this seemed to trigger a second round of depression and strange behaviors. She stopped talking, mutilated herself, obsessively read the Bible, and refused to feed her baby. Yates was hospitalized again and treated with antidepressants and the antipsychotic drugs that had been effective in the past. She was

Andrea Yates killed all five of her children in what one psychiatrist called "sever postpartum psychosis."

Andrea Yates began having serious postpartum depression following the birth of her fourth child.

released from the hospital, and her doctor slowly reduced her antipsychotic medication, finally cutting it off completely in early June. Believing that Yates was improving, on June 18, 2001, her doctor also abruptly reduced her dosage of an antidepressant medication and recommended she see a psychologist. Just two days later, on June 20, 2001, after her husband left for work and before her mother-in-law arrived to help care for the children, Yates carefully implemented her tragic plan of murder.

One Mother's Psychotic Break

Yates filled the bathtub with water and quickly drowned her three youngest sons, Luke, Paul, and John, then laid their bodies side by side on a bed. She then proceeded to drown her baby, Mary. While the baby was still in the tub, Yates' oldest boy, Noah, came into the bathroom and saw his sister's lifeless body. Realizing what was happening, Noah tried to run away but was chased by his mother and dragged screaming back to the bathroom, where he, too, was drowned despite a desperate struggle to survive. After all the children were dead, Yates placed the baby's body on the bed with her three brothers, covered them with a sheet, and left Noah's body face down in the tub. She calmly called the 911 emergency phone number and then her husband, telling him, "You need to come home. It's time. I did it." When he asked what she meant, she said, "It's the children." Now frightened, her husband asked, "Which one?" Yates replied, "All of them."[2]

Yates was taken into police custody where she confessed to killing her children. When asked why she did it, Yates explained that she felt she was a bad mother and that she needed to be punished. She later explained further that she believed the children were going to hell and she had to save them. A psychiatrist who examined Yates during this period concluded she was suffering from severe postpartum psychosis, an acute form of major depression often characterized by visual hallucinations, a disconnection from reality, and suicidal or homicidal thoughts. On July 31, 2001, Andrea Yates was indicted for capital murder. Her lawyers argued an insanity defense, but the jury rejected it and took only three hours on March 12, 2002, to find her guilty. The same jury, however, rejected the death penalty and instead gave her a life sentence. She was sent to a state psychiatric prison in Texas.

Three years later, on January 6, 2005, an appeals court overturned Yates' conviction on various legal grounds and ordered a new trial. At the second trial, Yates was found not guilty by reason of insanity and committed to a state mental hospital. Although she may be mentally ill the rest of her life, her status will be reviewed each year by the courts and any recommendation that she be released can be overruled by a judge.

Sad Cases Raise Awareness

The publicity surrounding the Andrea Yates case helped to educate people about postpartum depression and the potential for it to develop into a lethal psychosis. About one out of every thousand women develops postpartum psychosis, and more than five hundred cases of child homicide are reported each year in the United States. In Texas alone, since Andrea Yates' conviction, three other similar cases have hit the news: Lisa Ann Diaz was accused of drowning her two daughters; Deanna Laney admitted to killing her two sons by using rocks to bash in their skulls; and Dena Schlosser was charged with capital murder after cutting off her daughter's arm.

Deanna Laney admitted killing her two sons.

When Motherhood Becomes a Nightmare

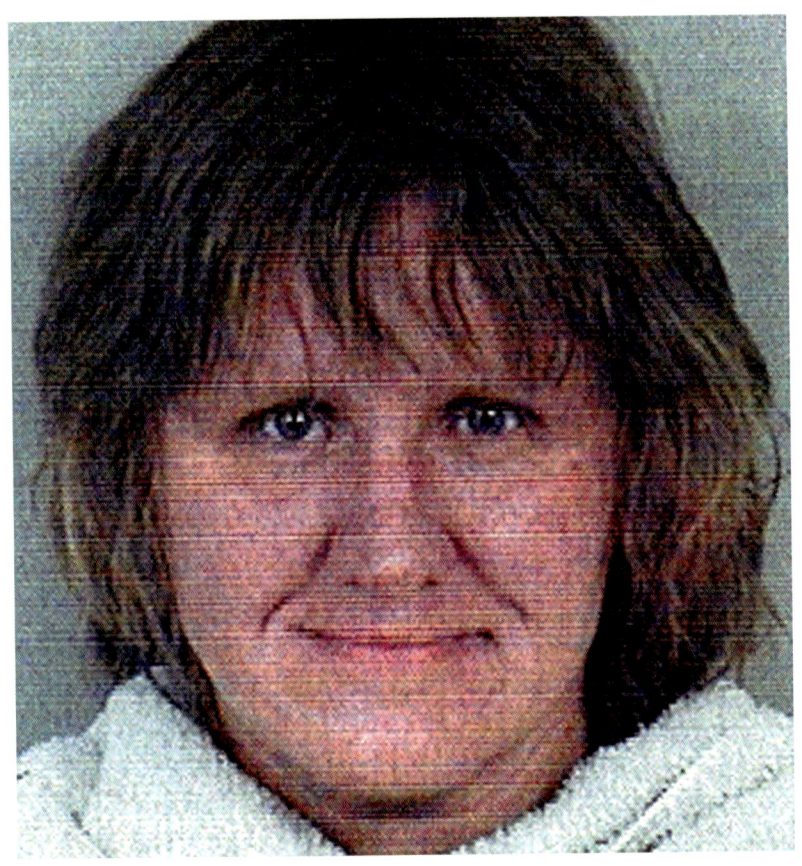

Dena Schlosser cut off her daughter's arm. The child later died.

Fortunately, the vast majority of mothers with postpartum depression do not develop psychotic behaviors or harm their children or themselves. Most simply suffer quietly with depression, unsure of where to turn for help. However, any type of depression in mothers can have other long-lasting effects on their children. Experts urge any woman who feels depressed after childbirth to immediately tell her doctor. For those who do seek help, there are medications and other treatments that have proven to be very effective. Prompt treatment, experts say, can help prevent potential harm and ensure a much brighter future—not only for mothers, but also for their children, their husbands, and others who may be affected.

CHAPTER ONE

What Is Postpartum Depression?

Experts estimate that up to 80 to 90 percent of women experience some type of mood disturbance or depression following pregnancy and childbirth. It is common for new mothers to feel sad, upset, afraid, or unloving toward their baby, as well as guilty for having these negative feelings. For one in every ten women, however, these feelings develop into major postpartum depression, or PPD. Although PPD is not yet fully understood by experts, it appears to be similar in many respects to other types of depression caused by irregularities in the brain's neurotransmitters. However, PPD is different from other mood disorders because it is believed to be triggered and complicated by hormonal fluctuations and other changes accompanying pregnancy and childbirth.

Levels of Postpartum Depression

The term postpartum depression is used to refer to many different types and levels of depression in new mothers. The mildest depressive condition following childbirth is often called the baby blues, a short-term period of heightened emotions that occurs within 48 hours of delivery and can last from one to two weeks. Women suffering from the baby blues typically feel sad, irritable, anxious, tired, and emotionally worn-out. They often cry more easily than normal and have difficulty sleeping.

What Is Postpartum Depression?

This condition is widespread; more than half of all women who give birth experience these temporary feelings of depression. But the baby blues usually are not severe enough to prevent a mother from caring for her baby, and most affected women eagerly solicit support from friends and family. The majority of women with this mild form of depression recover quickly without any medical or psychiatric intervention.

For about 10 to 17 percent of new mothers, however, depressive feelings run much deeper. These women fall into a more prolonged period of depression that can go on for months or even years. The characteristics of this illness are similar to those seen in baby blues—sadness, tearfulness, moodiness, fatigue, sleeping troubles, and impaired concentration—but are much more serious. Symptoms of serious PPD, for example, often include appetite problems, feelings of complete despair

It is common for women to experience depression or some kind of mood disturbance following pregnancy and childbirth.

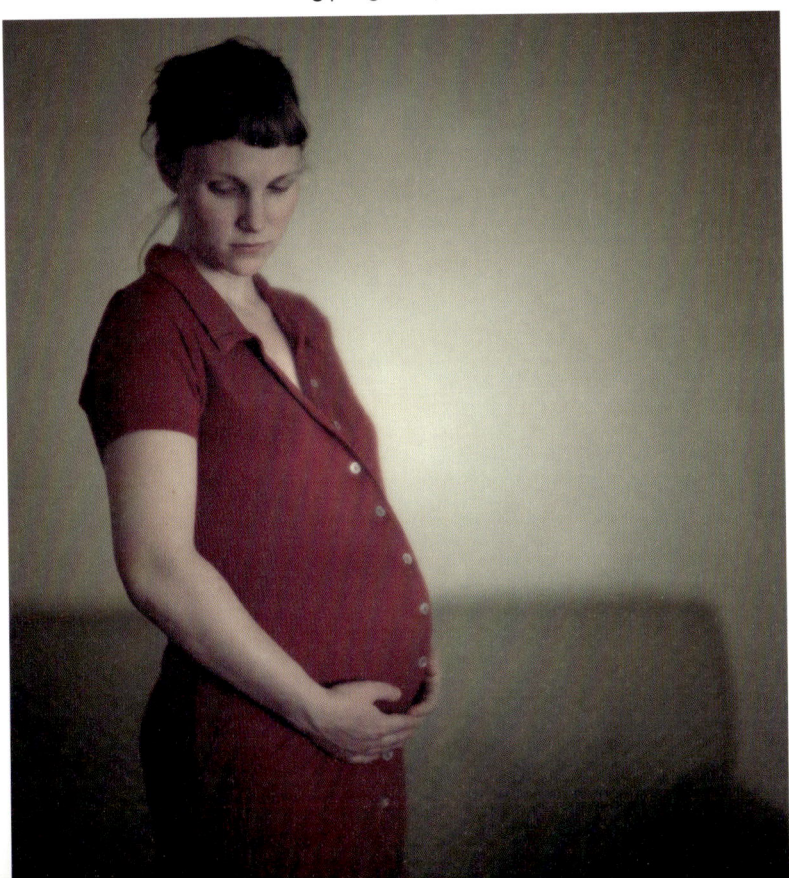

and hopelessness, suicidal thoughts, and continuing feelings of inadequacy as a parent.

The key feature of PPD, in fact, is a persistent feeling of deep depression so severe that it prevents a mother from taking care of her infant the way she and others expect. When suffering from major depression, mothers often feel detached from their newborns, not interested in breast-feeding, incapable of love, and unable to bond. The actress Brooke Shields described her feelings toward her baby during her bout with PPD in her book, *Down Came the Rain: My Journey Through Postpartum Depression*:

> My child was a source of joy to everyone who came into contact with her, except me. I couldn't believe I was missing out on all of the happiness they described and which I had so anticipated. I had been waiting to be overwhelmed

Brooke Shields wrote a book about her bout with postpartum depression.

by the deepest love fathomable, and all I felt was distance and dread. Nothing was as I had pictured it.[3]

PPD patients also tend to isolate from other people. They often feel profoundly ashamed of their feelings of disinterest in their child and sadness at a time when everyone expects them to be happy, and they are afraid to tell anybody about it.

Variations of Major Postpartum Depression

Despite the common thread of deep depression, however, PPD symptoms can vary greatly from person to person. Many women feel depressed all the time, while others experience swings in their moods. Some women feel excessive anxiety or worry. In fact, PPD patients can exhibit symptoms of various other recognized mental disorders, including anxiety, eating disorders, bipolar disorder, obsessive-compulsive disorder, or post-traumatic stress disorder. The *Diagnostic and Statistical Manual of Mental Disorders*, known as the *DSM-IV*, a manual published by the American Psychiatric Association that lists mental health disorders, does not even list a separate disorder called postpartum depression. Instead, the manual categorizes depressive disorders according to the specific symptoms and then adds information indicating that the condition develops in the postpartum period.

PPD patients with panic anxiety disorder, for example, may have panic attacks in addition to various other symptoms associated with major depression. Such attacks are characterized by symptoms such as heart palpitations or chest pain, shortness of breath, profuse sweating, trembling or tingling in various parts of the body, feelings of choking or nausea, dizziness, chills or hot flashes, and unexplained fear. Many people experience panic attacks only in certain places or situations where escape seems impossible, such as airplanes, bridges, tunnels, or elevators. This condition is known as agoraphobia. In other cases, the panic attacks seem to occur randomly, without any

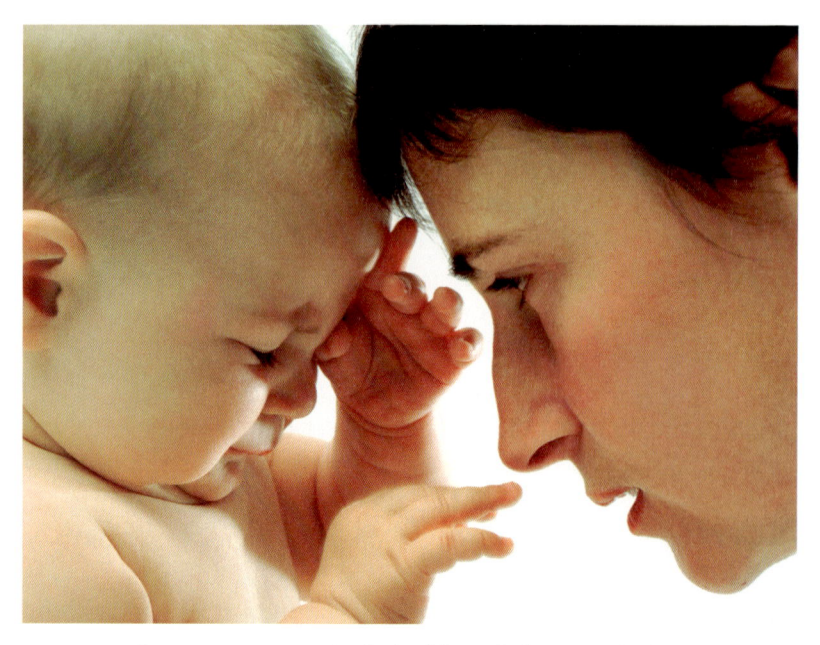

Many mothers experience the baby blues following the birth of their baby.

particular external stimulus. Sometimes, women first experience panic attacks during pregnancy. This increases their risk of having the same symptoms postpartum.

PPD patients with postpartum obsessive-compulsive disorder (OCD) tendencies, on the other hand, focus on specific fears, usually concerns that they might harm the baby. These thoughts are called obsessive when they are unwanted, repetitive, inappropriate, and distressing to the mother, and they are compulsive when they result in behaviors that she cannot stop or control. One woman's struggle with OCD is described on the Web site of Postpartum Support International, a PPD support group:

> Each time I went near the balcony I would clutch my baby tightly until I was in a room with the door closed. Only then did I know he was safe one more time from me dropping him over. The bloody scenes I would envision horrified me. Passing the steak knives in the kitchen triggered images of my stabbing the baby, so I asked my

Women and Depression

Depression strikes a surprising number of people, and women are even more prone than men to experience major depression at some point in their lives. Research has shown, for example, that about 19 million people in the United States—one in every ten adults—suffer from one form of depression or another. However, approximately 20 percent of women become depressed, while the percentage among men is only about 10 percent. In other words, a woman is about twice as likely as a man to develop depression sometime during her lifetime. A number of factors may explain this female vulnerability to depression. These include reproductive, hormonal, or genetic factors that are unique to women, or the fact that women tend to outlive men and then often live alone as isolated widows. Other possible reasons include the more frequent instances of sexual abuse experienced by women and the greater stresses placed on women to handle both work and home responsibilities. Women, too, are more likely to be poor than men, and this can contribute significantly toward feelings of depression.

husband to hide the knives. I never bathed my baby alone since I was afraid I might drown him. Although I didn't think I would ever really hurt my baby son, I never trusted myself alone with him. I was terrified I would "snap" and actually carry out one of these scary thoughts. If my baby got sick it would be all my fault, so I would clean and clean to make sure there were no germs. Although I had always been more careful than other people, now I would check the locks on the windows and doors many times a day.[4]

Surprisingly, negative, unacceptable thoughts about the baby are common even for healthy mothers. A recent study conduc-

The Role of Genetics

The risk for developing postpartum depression increases dramatically when there is a family history of the disease. Research has shown that a woman is up to three times more likely to suffer major depression if one or more first-degree relatives, such as a mother, father, or sibling, has been diagnosed with depression. And the risk is slightly higher if relatives have had bipolar disorder. This suggests that depression has a significant genetic component that allows daughters to inherit a predisposition toward depression that is triggered by a stressful event such as the birth of a child. For this reason, experts say it is important for pregnant women to tell their doctors about any type of family history with mental illness, so that they can be prepared to treat her if necessary. However, not everyone with a family history of depression develops postpartum depression; some women in this category never have any mental problems. Conversely, major depression also occurs in women who have no family members with the disease. Genetics, therefore, appears to be only one of the risk factors for depression among new mothers, along with other things such as biochemistry, stress, and psychological triggers.

ted by doctors at the Mayo Clinic, a world-renowned medical facility, examined the written thoughts of three hundred postpartum women who had no history of psychiatric problems and found several disturbing themes. As psychiatrist Shaila Kulkarni Misri explains, these themes included: "thoughts of suffocation ('Maybe my baby rolled over and died from SIDS'), thoughts of accidents ('I think of the neighbor's dog attacking my baby'), unwanted ideas of or urges toward intentional harm ('Would she be brain-damaged if I threw her out the window?'), thoughts of illness or losing the infant, unacceptable sexual thoughts, and finally contaminations."[5] For most women, these

What Is Postpartum Depression?

are passing thoughts that are quickly dismissed, but for those with OCD, the thoughts become more intense and are accompanied by compulsive actions, usually revolving around making sure the baby is clean, protected, and safe. Unfortunately, many women do not tell their doctors about obsessive thoughts of harm to their babies for fear that they will be declared unfit parents and have their children taken away.

Another anxiety disorder, post-traumatic stress disorder (PTSD), can be even more alarming for new mothers. This illness, known to afflict soldiers who have faced traumatic combat experiences, is one in which the person repeatedly re-experiences the traumatic event through terrible nightmares or daytime memory flashbacks. PTSD patients feel like they are actually reliving the event emotionally, and this causes them to become emotionally numb in order to escape the pain. This emotional numbing, however, can cause PTSD sufferers to isolate themselves from social encounters and avoid contact with family and friends, and they can eventually become hypersensitive to the slightest stimulation, exhibiting symptoms of extreme fear, breathing and heart problems, nausea, sweating, and feelings of panic.

Lance Corporal Blake Miller suffered from PTSD after serving in Iraq. Post-traumatic stress disorder can also affect new mothers.

New mothers who develop PTSD symptoms often are women who have experienced sexual violence, such as molestation or rape, earlier in their lives. Pregnancy, with all the required and repeated examinations of intimate body parts, can remind women of their earlier trauma and result in the onset of PTSD. In addition, for some women, there is evidence that the childbirth experience itself can induce PTSD symptoms postpartum. This is especially true if childbirth is painful or difficult, or if it is not a normal delivery and requires medical intervention, such as a Cesarian delivery where doctors must deliver the baby through surgery.

Other mental disorders are also triggered by pregnancy and childbirth, including eating disorders such as not eating enough food—a condition known as anorexia, or eating too much (bingeing) and then throwing up (purging)—a condition called bulimia. These disorders have recently gotten a lot of press atttention and are estimated to aflict 5 to 10 percent of young women. Many people believe that society's focus on unnatural thinness is damaging to a woman's sense of self-worth and contributes to these conditions. Studies have shown, however, that certain women have a greater likelihood of developing eating problems, most notably those with obsessively perfectionist, impulsive, risk-taking personalities. Whatever the cause, eating

Some women develop an eating disorder, such as anorexia, during pregnancy or after giving birth.

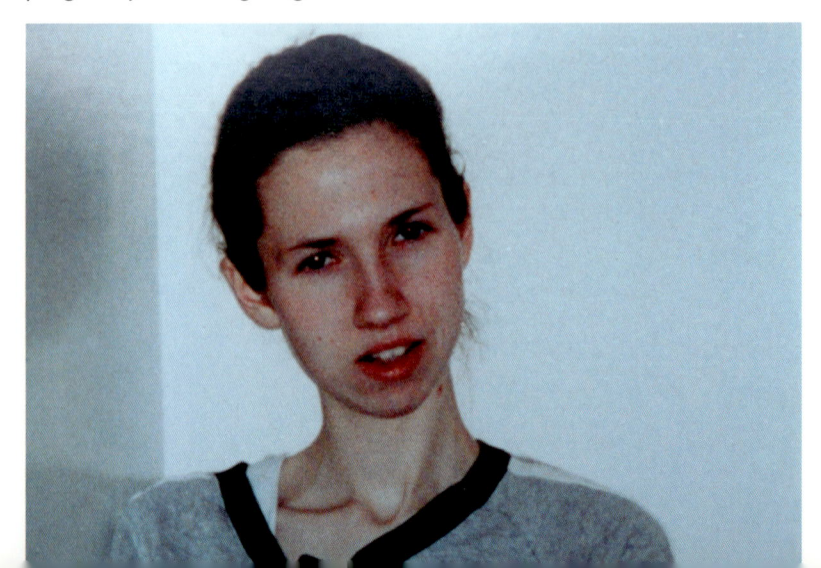

disorders during pregnancy tend to be very dangerous, both for the mother and the child, because neither is receiving proper nutrition. Some women are able to control their anorexia or bulimia during pregnancy but find that the disorder returns during the postpartum period, a time when nursing is vitally important to give the infant a good start in life. Sadly, some PPD mothers even restrict their children's food intake out of concern that their babies might get too fat.

Postpartum Psychosis

One particular type of PPD, called bipolar disorder or manic-depressive illness, is especially dangerous for mothers and their babies. In this condition, patients experience wild mood swings that range from deep despair to extreme happiness, or mania, when they have increased energy and zest for life. In between these extremes, patients may feel somewhat normal. Experts say women who have bipolar illness before they become pregnant are very likely to relapse after pregnancy and childbirth. In a small percentage of women—about one or two out of every thousand—their bipolar disease develops into a dangerous psychosis that requires immediate intervention and hospitalization. No one is really sure why some women cross this line into psychosis and others do not.

In this worst form of PPD, psychosis, patients experience hallucinations, delusions, despair or elation, extreme anxiety, and generally become cut off from reality and unable to control their thoughts, emotions, or actions. They hear voices or see things that simply are not there and hold illogical beliefs that defy common sense. Often, psychotic patients have suicidal or homicidal thoughts, and they frequently act upon them, putting both their lives and the lives of their children at serious risk. Experts say ordinary postpartum depression can turn into psychosis very quickly in bipolar women, before the women's partners or family see it coming. In these cases, it is very important for the woman to be hospitalized immediately at the first sign of severe mania, when most psychotic episodes of attempted suicide or homicide occur. Fortunately, incidents

About one in every five women will develop depression sometime during her lifetime.

of mothers actually killing or seriously harming their babies are relatively rare; according to Phillip J. Resnick, a doctor at Case Western Reserve University in Cleveland, "Of the mothers whose depression develops into psychosis, . . . [only] about 4% will harm their children if the psychosis is not treated."[6]

Biological Causes

No specific cause has been identified for any of these forms of PPD, and experts think that they all may be triggered by both biological and psychological factors. One biological factor that all depression disorders have in common, for example, is a dysfunction in brain chemicals that regulate mood. These chemicals, called neurotransmitters, create pathways between tens of billions of nerve cells in the human brain, called neurons, allowing them to communicate with each other. In this way, the brain controls all our thoughts, emotions, and actions. Five of these neurotransmitters have been linked with depression:

serotonin, norpinephrine, dopamine, acetylcholine, and gamma-aminobutyric acid (GABA). Imbalances of these chemicals seem to induce depressive symptoms, and restoration of the needed chemical, through drugs or other means, seems to relieve the depression. And these imbalances often have a genetic component; depression is much more likely if a parent, sibling, or grandparent suffered from the condition.

The body makes serotonin from an amino acid called tryptophan, and serotonin has the effect of making a person feel calm, happy, pain-free, and able to sleep well. Many experts have noted that the reason many people feel sleepy after eating a large Thanksgiving dinner is because turkey has high amounts of tryptophan, Tryptophan is also found in other foods, such as brown rice, peanuts, and soybeans. Norepinephrine, on the other hand, is a chemical used by the body to respond to stress with a "fight-or-flight" response, which causes the heart to beat faster and the lungs to breathe more deeply to help a person escape danger. Studies have shown that low amounts of norepinephrine can cause depressed feelings while high levels are associated with euphoric feelings or mania. The other three neurotransmitters linked with depression—dopamine, acetylcholine, and gamma-aminobutyric acid (GABA)—are related to various pleasure and relaxation centers in the brain. Low levels of these chemicals are believed to play a role in various depressive symptoms, including activities such as digestion, relaxation responses of the heart and lungs, and the ability to sleep.

Unlike forms of depression that strike men and non-pregnant women, however, PPD may also be triggered or exacerbated by the hormonal changes of pregnancy and childbirth. Hormones, like neurotransmitters, are chemicals produced by the body that affect mood. Three of the most important human hormones are estrogen (which regulates female sexual development, menstruation, and pregnancy), progesterone (a second female hormone that works in conjunction with estrogen), and testosterone (a hormone responsible for male sexual development, but which is also present in women to provide sexual desire). Another hormone, cortisol, is called the stress hormone because it is secreted by the body during stressful events to provide a burst of energy, increase immunity, reduce pain sensitivity, and heighten memory.

When a woman becomes pregnant, her neurotransmitters and hormones undergo a number of changes to help prepare her body for childbirth and motherhood. Hormones such as estrogen and progesterone, for example, are produced in higher amounts to help prepare the womb for pregnancy. Estrogen levels, in fact, increase to 130 times the normal levels and progesterone levels increase seven-fold. The higher amounts of estrogen, in turn, increase serotonin and norepinephrine levels in the brain, helping to produce a positive outlook during pregnancy. Other hormones such as cortisol are produced to aid in childbirth and nursing. Within forty-eight hours after childbirth, however, the levels of the hormones estrogen, progesterone, and cortisol fall dramatically, along with the levels of neurotransmitters such as serotonin and norepinephrine. Studies have suggested these drop-offs may play a large role in the onset of depression in postpartum women.

One study conducted in the United Kingdom, for example, found that women who were given estrogen for postpartum depression responded favorably, and other studies have suggested that the hormone might also prevent PPD. Research on progesterone, on the other hand, has shown that this hormone causes the breakdown of serotonin and contributes to negative mood changes during and after pregnancy. No one understands, however, why the interplay of neurotransmitters and hormones in some women appears to trigger depression and mood problems, while in other women it does not.

Psychological Risk Factors

A variety of psychological, social, and emotional factors comprise the third component believed to play an important role in PPD. Previous mental health or addiction problems, especially during pregnancy, are a major warning sign that similar problems might develop postpartum. Social problems such

What Is Postpartum Depression?

Social problems (financial, educational, relationship, etc.) may increase the likelihood that a pregnant woman will develop PPD.

as poverty or financial concerns, unemployment, inadequate housing, low educational levels, a lack of social support, or similar survival issues also make it much more likely that a woman will become depressed. Recent stressful events, such as the death of a family member, a serious illness, marital discord, or domestic violence, can also put a new mother more at risk of developing PPD.

Other common psychological issues that can help trigger PPD involve the mother's emotional reaction to her pregnancy. If the pregnancy is unwanted or preceded by one or more miscarriages or abortions, or if the pregnancy is uncomfortable or accompanied by medical difficulties or anxieties, mothers may spiral downward into depression. In other cases, the pregnancy is fine but the birth itself is traumatic in some way that triggers feelings of sadness or anxiety. Still other women sink into depression only after the birth. The reality of motherhood can bring reduced independence and social status for stay-at-home moms. Many feel increased isolation from the daily, sometimes tedious, regimen of taking care of the baby. Likewise, most new mothers get inadequate sleep. The lack of close-by family support for new mothers in today's modern society may also be a contributing factor.

The Role of Nutrition

Even if PPD is triggered by some combination of neurological, hormonal, and psychological factors, some researchers believe that, for at least some women, the root cause of PPD may be malnutrition and nutrient depletion, or in some cases, an excess of certain nutrients. Nutritionist Dean Raffelock explains:

> The scientific consensus is that PPD is multi-factorial, which means that all of the above variables—hormonal, psychological, and neurochemical—come into play. . . . [But] the balance of each of these systems relies upon proper nutrition. If the nutritional building blocks that the body needs to make hormones, neurotransmitters, and other mood-altering body chemicals are not present in adequate amounts, mood and physical health can both be compromised.[7]

Underlying problems might include vitamin, mineral, or amino acid deficiencies. One condition, anemia, for example, is characterized by a dearth of red blood cells caused by a deficiency of iron, vitamin B-12, or folic acid. In other cases, nutrient deficiencies disable the body from making enough of one or more of the neurotransmitters, hormones, or other substances that work together to moderate mood. A number of women with PPD, for example, have been found to have hypothyroidism, a condition caused by the thyroid gland's production of insufficient amounts of the hormone thyroxin due to a lack of iodine. Studies have also shown that women with PPD tend to have elevated levels of copper, an essential mineral but one that, in excess, is believed to alter the balance of dopamine and norepinephrine, two of the brain's neurotransmitters. Since copper levels typically more than double during pregnancy, then drop off after childbirth, scientists speculate that PPD may be caused when copper levels fail to normalize in the postpartum period, possibly because of a flaw in the protein that regulates copper levels.

One day, researchers may be better able to pinpoint the causes so that women can better prevent the agony of PPD. Until then, however, the most important advice from doctors is for mothers to immediately report any symptoms or history of depression or anxiety. Misri notes that,

> Being aware of a women's psychiatric history is as important as knowing any other aspect of her medical history. Unrecognized and untreated depression—whether or not it is accompanied by the complications of anxiety disorder, post-traumatic stress disorder, or an eating disorder—can compromise that positive outcome as surely as any undiagnosed physical condition.[8]

CHAPTER TWO

Diagnosis and Drug Treatment

PPD has long been downplayed and misunderstood by doctors and dismissed within our culture, but today more is being learned about how to diagnose and treat the disorder. Almost all experts agree that the key is encouraging women to overcome societal or cultural stigmas and report symptoms early, so that they can be adequately assessed by professionals and treated before enduring months or years of depression that can pose health and safety risks for both mothers and children. Once the depressive condition is diagnosed, the most common treatment is a medical one that employs antidepressants and other drugs to return brain chemicals and hormones to their proper levels.

Obstacles to Diagnosis

The first step for women experiencing depression that lasts longer than a couple of weeks after childbirth is to seek help, but this is not as easy as it sounds. Sometimes, it is very difficult for a new mother or those around her to recognize the symptoms of depression. Indeed, depression sometimes causes physical symptoms, such as back pain, headaches, shortness of breath, stomach or intestinal problems, or leg and joint pain, that might be viewed by the average person as having a physi-

Diagnosis and Drug Treatment

cal cause and would not be considered signs of a mental illness. And these symptoms often do not occur all at once, but present themselves sporadically over time, along with slowly mounting feelings of sadness or anxiety. As psychiatrist Shaila Kulkarni Misri explains,

> If you break a bone or scald yourself with boiling water, there is immediate acute pain, and the source of that pain is instantly apparent. Depression, however, doesn't present itself with such obvious and immediate symptoms. Rather, the mental and physical changes it causes creep up gradually, sometimes over a period of years, eating away at and eroding one's quality of life, and very often

A complete medical history, including psychiatric as well as physical, is important for both the mother and the baby.

the person who is suffering is the last to recognize what's happening to . . . her.[9]

Many women also hide their feelings of depression out of shame and fear that they will be viewed as bad mothers. Yale University School of Medicine professor C. Neill Epperson explains, "Societal pressures to be a 'good mother' are such that if a woman does recognize that something is wrong, she is loath to admit it."[10] Also, most cultures see the birth of a child as a joyful occasion, and mothers who do not feel joyful often mask their true feelings in order to conform to the expectations of their spouses, family, friends, and society. Similarly, mothers are especially reluctant to admit to any type of mental illness because they fear they might be locked up in a mental hospital or institution or that their child might be taken away by the authorities. This is especially true for women who are experiencing thoughts or fears about harming their babies.

Even if postpartum women do seek help for depression, doctors and even family members and friends often minimize the severity of their symptoms, believing them to be short-term blues or the result of lack of sleep or the hormonal adjustments that naturally follow childbirth. After all, a woman who recently gave birth quite often struggles with issues such as a lack of energy, fatigue, inability to sleep, or loss of appetite—all problems that can also point to PPD. It is not surprising, therefore, that it is sometimes difficult even for doctors to separate normal postpartum stresses from serious depression.

Diagnosing Postpartum Depression

Moreover, if PPD is suspected, physicians are not able to diagnose PPD with a single medical test. Typically, however, health care professionals start by administering the Edinburgh Postnatal Depression Scale (EPDS), a questionnaire developed by doctors in the United Kingdom to help primary care physicians detect PPD. The questionnaire consists of the following ten

Diagnosis and Drug Treatment

statements, and patients are asked to circle any responses that represent feelings they had within the last seven days:

1. I have been able to laugh and see the funny side of things.
   As much as I always could
   Not quite so much now
   Definitely not so much now
   Not at all

2. I have looked forward with enjoyment to things.
   As much as I ever did
   Rather less than I used to
   Definitely less than I used to
   Hardly at all

3. I have blamed myself unnecessarily when things went wrong.
   Yes, most of the time
   Yes, some of the time
   Not very often
   No, never

4. I have been anxious or worried for no good reason.
   No, not at all
   Hardly ever
   Yes, sometimes
   Yes, very often

5. I have felt scared or panicky for no very good reason.
   Yes, quite a lot
   Yes, sometimes
   No, not much
   No, not at all

6. Things have been getting on top of me.
   Yes, most of the time I haven't been able to cope at all
   Yes, sometimes I haven't been coping as well as usual
   No, most of the time I have coped quite well
   No, I have been coping as well as ever

7. I have been so unhappy that I have had difficulty sleeping.
   Yes, most of the time
   Yes, sometimes
   Not very often
   No, not at all

8. I have felt sad or miserable.
   Yes, most of the time
   Yes, quite often
   Not very often
   No, not at all

9. I have been so unhappy that I have been crying.
   Yes, most of the time
   Yes, quite often
   Only occasionally
   No, never

10. The thought of harming myself has occurred to me.
    Yes, quite often
    Sometimes
    Hardly ever
    Never

The patient's responses are scored from 0 to 3 depending on the severity of symptoms, and then all scores are added together to arrive at a total score. According to the questionnaire's creators, if the total score is above 92.3 percent, the patient is likely

Celebrities with Postpartum Depression

Historically, postpartum depression has been a hidden disease that women did not discuss publicly. In recent years, however, a number of Hollywood celebrities have rebelled against this stigma and openly revealed that they became severely depressed following childbirth. Marie Osmond, a singer and television personality known for her bright smile and bubbly personality, was one of the first celebrities to break the silence. In 2001, she wrote a book about the depression that followed the birth of her seventh child (*Behind the Smile: My Journey Out of Postpartum Depression*). Brooke Shields, the famous model and actress, followed suit in 2005 with the publication of her book, *Down Came the Rain: My Journey Through Postpartum Depression*, detailing the debilitating depression she suffered after giving birth to her first child, Rowan. Courtney Cox, star of the TV show, *Friends*, also went public about her battle with depression in 2005, a year after her daughter Coco was born. Most recently, some observers have suggested that pop singing diva Britney Spears, who has been partying heavily since her break-up with husband Kevin Federline, may be struggling with postpartum depression and using drugs and alcohol as a way to self-medicate.

Brooke Shields, top, and Courtney Cox both went public with their PPD.

One Woman's Story

The story of Tonya Rosenberg's battle with postpartum depression, excerpted below, was posted on a PPD support Web site:

> The birth was largely uneventful.... Back home, things deteriorated.... I was exhausted, but couldn't sleep. I was hyper alert to... [my baby Emily] at all times. She slept in the bed with me for nursing purposes, so I never ever slept deeply. I went days without bathing. I had no appetite, but breast-feeding was something I was determined to do and I had to eat to produce milk. I was afraid to leave the house... what I was afraid of I'm not exactly sure.... After some time, I guess I "snapped."... I "saw" myself taking this little angel by the ankles and smashing her against the wall until it ran red.... [I] called my [doctor and]... was put on Prozac.... I lucked out, and Prozac worked really well for me.... My then-husband tried his best, but the damage was already done, and we divorced when Emily was 3 years old.

Tonya Rosenberg, "Life Handed Me Lemons, But I'm Making Lemonade Today," PPD Support Page, undated. www.ppdsupportpage.com/tonya.html.

---

to be suffering from a depressive illness. Although it seems almost too simple, this questionnaire has been highly effective at identifying women suffering from major depression.

The EPDS, however, is just a screening tool, and if a patient scores high on the questionnaire, experts say a comprehensive health assessment is necessary to rule out any other possible medical conditions, to assess stress and depression levels, and to develop an effective treatment plan. A medical assessment, for example, can determine whether symptoms of depression might be caused by conditions such as reactions to or side effects of medication that might have been taken during pregnancy. One particular drug, metoclopramide (which is sold under the brand name Reglan), is often prescribed to women to help control the nausea and vomiting that are common during pregnancies, but doctors have found that it causes depression in some women.

Depression could also be the result of physical problems such as anemia, a condition that deprives the body of oxygen needed to function properly and which can be the result of a diet low in B vitamins or iron. Pregnant women are especially vulnerable to anemia, due to the depletion of nutrients caused by the growing fetus, and the loss of large amounts of blood during childbirth can further deplete essential vitamins and minerals. Thyroid disorders, too, are common, affecting 4 to 10 percent of postpartum women. The thyroid gland controls the body's metabolism rate and immune system, and the levels of hormones produced by the thyroid change during pregnancy to keep the mother's body from attacking the fetus. After childbirth, some women experience problems getting the thyroid function to return to normal.

Moreover, depression after childbirth can be the result of underlying diseases, such as diabetes, infectious disease, hepatitis, mononucleosis, or acquired immune deficiency syndrome (AIDS). From 3 to 5 percent of pregnant women in the United States, for example, are diagnosed with gestational diabetes, a special form of diabetes in which the effects of insulin (a hormone produced by the body to convert sugar, starch, and other foods into energy) are blocked by estrogen and other hormones during pregnancy.

Another part of this health assessment is a thorough interview of the patient covering a wide range of health-related topics. This will help doctors learn about the patient's and her family's medical history, whether she or any blood relative has previously suffered from depression, the status of her marriage and other relationships, her level of stress, and the amount of social support available to her. In addition, the interview should enable doctors to assess other important issues such as the patient's sleep and eating patterns; her feelings about the pregnancy, delivery, and motherhood; her level of anxiety and depression; and whether she entertains suicidal or homicidal thoughts.

A Treatment Plan

At its conclusion, this thorough health assessment should produce a diagnosis and recommendations for treatment. Ideally, both the assessment and the treatment of PPD incorporates a team approach that can include not only the woman's obstetrician or family physician, but also a psychiatrist, who plots an overall mental health strategy and who specializes in PPD drug treatment, and psychologists or therapists who will monitor the patient on a regular basis and who specialize in PPD cases and in teaching parenting skills.

The treatment plan for PPD typically includes prescription drugs, often combined with some type of psychotherapy or counseling. Although many women resist taking drugs, most experts agree for a variety of reasons that medication is often

Medications are necessary to restore balance to brain chemistry and return hormones to normal levels in women with PPD.

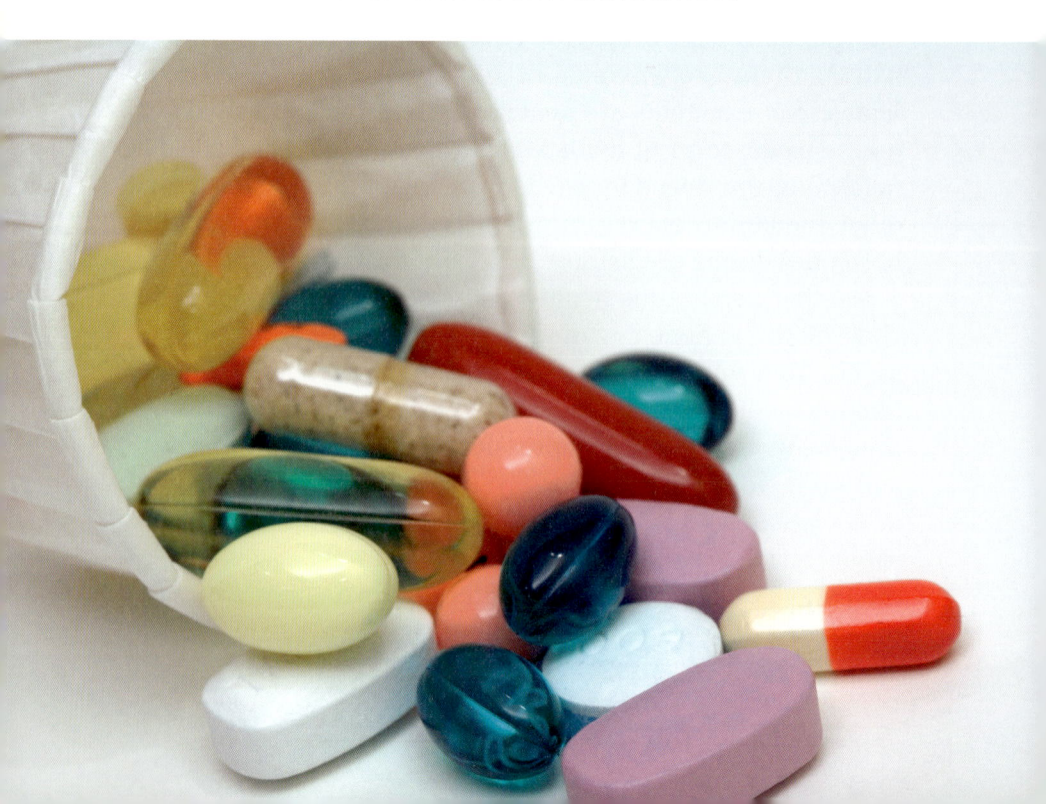

necessary, especially for more severe forms of PPD. As PPD experts Ronald Rosenberg, Deborah Greening, and James Windell explain,

> If your symptoms are so severe that you are having trouble taking care of yourself and your baby, if you have frequent thoughts about harming your baby, or if you're having suicidal thoughts, then most certainly medication will be the cornerstone of your treatment."[11]

Medications may include a variety of different drugs, all of which are designed to restore balance to brain chemistry and return hormones to normal levels. The drug prescriptions vary from woman to woman, because each person reacts a bit differently to the same medication. Drugs also often take time to work, and doctors may have to try different medications and dosages before arriving at one that will elicit the best response, with the fewest side effects, for each particular patient.

Antidepressant Drugs

The most widely used drug medications for PPD are antidepressants, which are designed specifically to target the dysfunctions in brain neurotransmitters that are believed to cause depressive symptoms. Although there are a variety of antidepressant drugs available, four main types are most frequently prescribed for major depression: trycyclics (TCAs), monoamine oxidase inhibitors (MAOIs), selective serotonin reuptake inhibitors (SSRIs), and serotonin norepinephrine reuptake inhibitors (SNRIs).

TCAs were first developed in the 1950s, and some drugs in this class are still used for certain types of major depression, such as OCD and panic disorders. They affect two chemical neurotransmitters, serotonin and norepinephrine, but they have significant side effects, are not tolerated as well by women, and can be toxic in large doses. For these reasons, they are now used infrequently in treating PPD. MAOIs, too, are avoided in postpartum situations for similar reasons. Instead, the two remaining antidepressants, SSRIs and SNRIs, are most likely to be prescribed to treat PPD.

SSRIs were introduced in the late 1980s and quickly became very popular in the United States because they had few side effects and appeared to be both effective and safe. Many people have heard of some of the most widely prescribed SSRI drugs, such as fluoxetine (sold under the brand name Prozac), sertraline (Zoloft), citalopram (Celexa), and paroxetine (Paxil). Prozac is one of the first SSRI drugs developed, and it continues to be frequently used to treat PPD. These drugs work primarily by increasing the levels of serotonin, a brain chemical that helps to elevate mood and improve a patient's appetite and ability to sleep. Although SSRIs are very effective at reducing PPD symptoms; however, they do not always completely eliminate all depressive symptoms, as TCA drugs can do. As a result, SNRIs were developed. These drugs affect norepinephrine neurotransmitters and are quite new, but several, including venlafaxine (Effexor) and duloxetine (Cymbalta), appear to achieve a complete remission of depression symptoms in postpartum women similar to the effectiveness levels of TCAs.

Drug Combinations

Depending on the type or severity of PPD symptoms, other drugs may be used in combination with antidepressants as part of the postpartum treatment plan. These include anticonvulsants, atypical antipsychotics, benzodiazepines, psychostimulants, hormones, and mood stabilizers. Women who are very depressed are usually desperate to feel better as quickly as possible, and for this reason doctors may prescribe a second medication that is known to act quickly to ease depression symptoms while waiting for another, perhaps more effective, medication to take full effect. At one time, so-called anticonvulsant drugs were used to get this quick mood lift for patients, but many of these were found to be potentially toxic to the liver, so they have become much less popular among doctors. More recently, antipsychotic medications, such as olanzapine (Zyprexa), quetiapine (Seroquel), and risperidone (Risperdal), are used to get the same short-term anti-depressive effect with fewer side effects.

Yet another category of medications, called benzodiazepines, have shown great success in treating anxiety. Included in this category are some relatively well-known drugs such as diazepam (Valium), alprazolam (Xanax), clonazepam (Klonopin), and zolpidem (Ambien). Although benzodiazepines have serious drawbacks, such as a tendency to cause drowsiness and create addiction if abused or taken for a long period of time, they act very quickly and can be used on a short-term, "as needed" basis to help women afflicted with severe anxiety or panic attacks. Benzodiazepines and the various other medications mentioned above have been shown to help patients sleep, reduce their anxiety, and fairly dramatically reduce their depression until even more effective antidepressants can take hold.

Two other types of medications are also frequently used by physicians in conjunction with antidepressants. One is psychostimulants, which are medications often thought of as "speed" drugs, but which can be very useful to PPD sufferers if used correctly. This category of medication helps with a patient's depression symptoms, while boosting energy and decreasing the sleepiness, lethargy, and fatigue that often accompanies PPD. Finally, hormone medications, such as patches that can be worn on the arm to supply extra estrogen, have been found to be very useful when combined with antidepressant drug treatment.

Bipolar and Psychotic Drug Treatments

For women with bipolar PPD, mood stabilizers are the most commonly prescribed medication. One of the oldest mood stabilizer drugs is Lithium, a metallic element that doctors in the late 1800s found would calm people's agitated moods. In 1970, Lithium was finally approved for use by the U.S. Food and Drug Administration (FDA), but it was not until 1990 that researchers learned exactly how the drug works—by affecting glutamate, one of the brain's neurotransmitters. Lithium, however, has been linked to heart defects in fetuses and infants and can be a very dangerous drug if used during pregnancy or while breast-feeding. Still, for postpartum women who are not breast feeding, it remains one of the most effective medications for treating bipolar disorders.

Treatment for the most serious PPD symptoms, such as postpartum psychosis, meanwhile, can require immediate treatment with several medications, including both antipsychotic agents and mood stabilizers such as Lithium. Severely psychotic patients may also require electroconvulsive therapy (ECT), the use of electric current to alter the electro-chemical processes in the brain. Although ECT often suggests negative associations to the average person, experts say in certain cases it can quickly cure debilitating delusions and hallucinations common in psychotic patients. Dr. Shaila Kulkarni Misri explains,

> Simply mentioning ECT immediately conjures up images of terrifying scenes from *One Flew Over the Cuckoo's Nest* and *A Beautiful Mind* [two popular movies in which ECT was depicted as crude and inhumane]. But ECT plays an important role in the treatment of psychiatric illness, and these movie scenes bear no resemblance to the reality of how it is administered today in a hospital setting. . . . Having used ECT on many patients both during pregnancy and postpartum, and having seen them recover dramatically without prolonged suffering, I can say with confidence that in those cases it was the correct choice of treatment.[12]

Misri, for example, tells the story of one postpartum patient, Peggy, who had become psychotic and delusional following the birth of her baby, Alicia. Misri explains:

> [Peggy] believed the baby was a monster and was telling her that she was a bad person. Every time Alicia cried, Peggy had thoughts of wanting to harm her. . . . Because she was considered to be a risk to herself and others . . . she was admitted to the hospital involuntarily with her

Diagnosis and Drug Treatment

husband's consent and received ECT. After the fourth treatment, she began to improve dramatically, to the point where she was able to hold her baby.... Her confusion and memory loss disappeared after a few months and she was able to establish a normal, loving relationship with her daughter.[13]

Overall, drug therapy (sometimes supplemented with ECT) has been proven to be a highly effective way to snap new mothers out of what could be devastating depression that could rob them, their babies, and their families of the many joys brought by having children. Although most medical doctors would like to avoid using drugs on postpartum women, experts say that drugs may be necessary before patients can start to benefit from other, non-drug treatments. PPD expert Dr. Sandra L. Wheatley argues,

> Surely it would be better for a women to have antidepressant [or other] medication[s] to help lift her mood so that she can then take full part in any therapy or counseling she is offered? ... Witnessing many women battling postnatal depression over the years has taught me this.[14]

Indeed, many experts say the alternative—avoiding drug treatment—would doom many postpartum women to despair, or at the very least, to a much slower recovery from depression. Refusal to be treated in serious cases could even result in forced hospitalization, the worst case scenario for all involved, but one that might be necessary for proper treatment and to protect the child.

CHAPTER THREE

Nondrug Therapies

Many experts believe that a combination of medication and psychotherapy is the most effective PPD strategy, because it addresses both the physical and the psychological/social aspects of depression. Women suffering from depression during the postpartum period, however, sometimes choose not to take drugs, and opt instead for psychotherapy, counseling, or other alternative therapies to resolve their PPD. In some cases, especially milder forms of depression, many doctors agree that psychological counseling alone can support a patient and help her to recover from depression. The verdict on other alternative treatments, such as herbs, vitamin supplements, and acupuncture, is undecided, but some people believe they also can be useful in treating some postpartum symptoms.

Psychotherapy Treatment

Although research has shown that PPD is linked to physical problems, such as imbalances in brain chemicals or hormones, the evidence is also clear that social and emotional factors contribute to feelings of depression. Experts agree, therefore, that it is just as important to address these psychological issues as it is to remedy biological problems. For this reason, doctors treating postpartum women struggling with depression usually suggest psychotherapy, in addition to drug treatment. As PPD experts Ronald Rosenberg, Deborah Greening, and James Windell emphatically put it, "Psychotherapy is not just an optional ingredient in the treatment of postpartum depression.

Nondrug Therapies

It is a necessity—particularly if you want the best and most expedient recovery."[15]

Psychotherapy, called "talk therapy," essentially refers to various types of professional counseling. Most typically, PPD counseling will mean one-on-one, individual counseling sessions between the patient and a therapist, but it also can include group therapy, marital or family counseling, or counseling to treat special problems that might have arisen during the postpartum period. The key is to match the individual patient with the type of therapy that will be most useful to her.

Although many people think of therapy as a long process that delves deeply into a patient's past, that is often not the case, especially with PPD cases. Dr. Shaila Kulkarni Misri explains,

> The traditional image many people have of talk therapy is of someone lying on a couch, dredging up memories from childhood, while a bearded doctor sits in a chair behind the patient's head, almost totally silent and certainly out of sight. In fact, however, most psychotherapists dealing with an acutely depressed patient . . . will initially focus on the present in order to help the patient solve his or her immediate problem."[16]

Herbal supplements and acupuncture are two examples of "alternative medicines" to treat symptoms of depression.

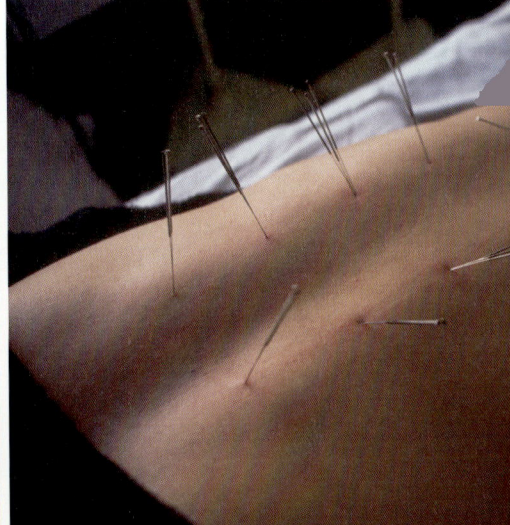

In cases of PPD, for example, most therapists would try to help the patient: (1) understand what behaviors and emotions contribute to depression; (2) address life issues such as relationship difficulties or other problems that may present obstacles to recovery; and (3) learn coping techniques that can be used to minimize stress or fears created by these social or emotional problems. Other issues that might be discussed are the patient's sleep patterns, the positive influence of exercise and proper diet, and the need for increasing social support systems.

Types of Psychotherapy

Individual PPD therapy can take one of several forms. One of the most commonly used types of therapy for depression is called cognitive behavior therapy (CBT). This technique combines cognitive therapy, which helps to change thinking patterns, with behavioral therapy, which focuses on changing behavior that may be contributing to depression. For example, CBT might be used in the case of a postpartum woman with anxiety and obsessive-compulsive tendencies to help her reduce or change her obsessive thoughts and to stop her from acting out in compulsive ways. To accomplish these gains, the CBT therapist typically meets with the patient on a regular basis, perhaps once or twice a week, for a relatively short time (typically, a period of twelve to sixteen weeks).

Another type of individual therapy often employed with PPD patients is interpersonal psychotherapy (IPT), a treatment that seeks to improve the patient's self-esteem and communication skills with family members and friends. IPT is especially appropriate for PPD patients who are dealing with feelings of loss or grief, the stress of negative relationships with spouses or other loved ones, or problems with lack of social support. This brand of therapy is often useful for women who reject antidepressant medications, because it has been shown as a relatively short-term way to reduce depressive conditions and increase social adjustment for postpartum women.

Psychodynamic psychotherapy, a third kind of individual therapy, is unlike CBT or IPT because instead of working only

Bright Light Therapy

Increasingly, psychiatrists, family doctors, and psychologists are using light therapy, a technique developed in the 1980s, to treat some forms of depression. The light therapy system consists of a box containing several high-intensity fluorescent light bulbs behind a diffusing screen, which can be set up on a table or desk top. To receive treatment, the patient sits close to the light box, eyes open, but not looking directly at the lights. Many people read, write, or eat during the treatment, which can last anywhere between fifteen minutes and three hours. This therapy has been found to be particularly successful with Seasonal Affective Disorder (SAD), a type of depression suffered during winter, but it also may be useful for postpartum depression. Most patients see improvement in their symptoms within a week with daily treatments, but treatments must continue to maintain the improved mood and energy levels. No one knows exactly how light therapy works, but it may reduce levels of the hormone melatonin, which creates a feeling of lethargy and sleepiness. The only serious side effect is that, in rare cases, the therapy may cause a person to become overactive or unable to sleep.

on present-day postpartum problems, it focuses on identifying negative patterns from a patient's past life that may be responsible for postpartum depression. In fact, short-term psychodynamic psychotherapy is largely used as a replacement for the long-term psychoanalysis that most people think of when they think of psychological therapy. This therapy, experts say, can be useful when a patient is repeating negative mothering patterns that she learned from her mother or when other past experiences are causing depression or inappropriate behaviors in the mother-child relationship.

In addition to or sometimes in place of individual therapy, therapists may recommend group therapy, in which six or more women meet as a group to share their problems and experiences with PPD. This type of support from other people who are going through the same postpartum difficulties often helps depressed patients to understand that they are not alone and that there is hope for recovery. Group therapy can be particularly helpful to women who lack a strong social support system. Misri notes that "The group environment actually functions to create a 'family' whom [postpartum women] . . . can trust and in whom they can confide without feeling ashamed, being embarrassed, or fearing that they will be belittled."[17] Sometimes, this type of support can also be found through postpartum public interest groups, some of which provide information or access to telephone or Internet support groups on their Web sites.

In many cases, postpartum women suffering from depression problems can also benefit from couples or family therapy. Depression can place huge stresses on families and marriages, and family therapy can bring husbands, older children, and close family members into the therapy sessions to help them

Parenting classes may be helpful in lending support to PPD sufferers.

understand and cope with symptoms of PPD. This therapy tries to reduce family conflict and shows family members positive ways of supporting the PPD mother while she is recovering from her depression.

Sometimes the therapist may also recommend parenting classes to lend further support to PPD mothers. During these sessions, new parents can learn techniques for taking care of and disciplining the child, and are given the opportunity to communicate with each other to share ideas and feelings about parenthood.

Sometimes, too, the hormonal and other changes of childbirth will trigger new problems or exacerbate old problems, such as alcohol/substance abuse or eating disorders. These behaviors can be extremely toxic for the health of both mother and baby, and they require their own specialized type of counseling. In whatever combination, all of these psychotherapies can be a huge help in reducing the stress and increasing the psychological support for women struggling with PPD.

Herbal Supplements

In addition to psychotherapy, postpartum women who reject taking drugs to ease their symptoms of depression are increasingly turning to alternative medicine, a broad term that refers to a host of unconventional treatments that are seen as alternatives to the various drugs offered by doctors trained in Western medical techniques.

One of these alternative therapies involves the use of herbs to treat diseases, including PPD and other forms of depression. Although there are a number of herbs known to have an effect on depression, probably the most popular anti-depression herb is Hypericum perforatum, more commonly known as St. John's Wort, a wild, yellow-flowering weed common in the United States and other places. St. John's Wort has been extensively researched, and many studies have found it to be effective for treating mild to moderate depression (but not for major depression). It also is well-tolerated by many people, inexpensive, and widely available in health food stores.

Just because herbs are natural, however, does not mean they are always safe. Experts warn that patients must make certain to tell their physicians if they are taking St. John's Wort or other herbs because they can interfere with other prescribed medications. St. John's Wort, for example, is known to reduce the effectiveness of certain drugs, such as birth control pills and some heart medications. It also can cause side effects, such as sensitivity to the sun, increased blood pressure, stomach upsets, allergic reactions, and fatigue (with long-term use). Because of the potential harm, some physicians adamantly oppose the use of herbal medicines for postpartum women. PPD experts Ronald Rosenberg, Deborah Greening, and James Windell warn,

> Don't fool yourself by believing that you're not taking medication when you take an herb. Even if it's advertised as being 'all natural,' if an herb has a drug effect, it will also have a drug-like side effect. We don't mix medications and herbs because the potential for interaction is high.... Our bottom line is that we are not going to 'play around with herbs' in pregnancy or in the treatment of postpartum depression.[18]

Nutritional Supplements

Nutritional supplements are also an alternative treatment for PPD recommended by some health practitioners. In fact, advocates of this course of treatment claim that drug therapy can dangerously deplete the body's reserves and that proper nutrition is the key to solving some cases of PPD. Nutritionist Dean Raffelock explains,

> In the vast majority of cases of PPD that are related to low serotonin or norepinephrine levels in the brain, the underlying cause is a deficiency of the nutritional precursors that the body needs to make these neurotransmitters. Interestingly, not only do the psychiatric drugs most commonly prescribed for PPD not increase serotonin and

Nondrug Therapies

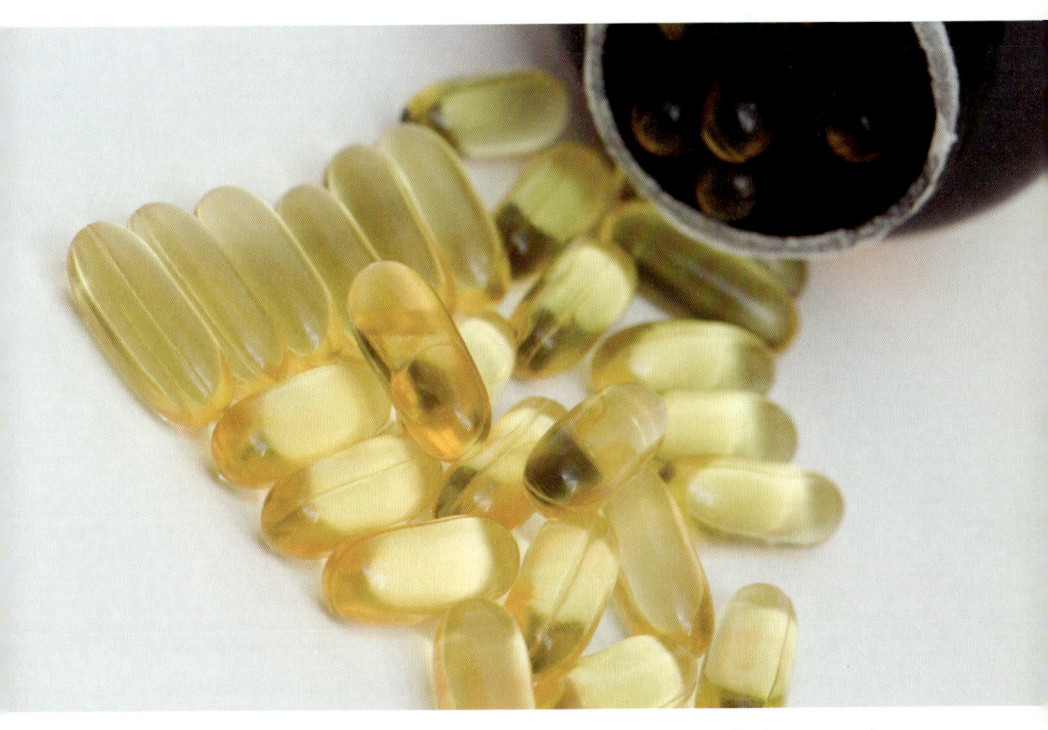

Nutritional supplements, some health practitioners believe, are key to the treatment of depression.

norepinephrine levels, but they actually cause the body's reserves of the nutritional precursors needed to produce them to be used up more rapidly, worsening the state of nutritional deficiency.[19]

According to this view, many cases of PPD can be effectively treated with a combination of hormones, vitamins and minerals, and in some cases, supplements to aid in the functioning of the adrenal and thyroid glands.

In fact, there is some evidence linking low levels of certain nutrients with depression. Studies suggest, for example, that many people with depression are deficient in folate (vitamin B9). These patients tend to be the most depressed, and they also may be less responsive to some of the SSRI antidepressant drugs. Doctors may begin by recommending a multivitamin

Vitamins for Postpartum Depression

Some doctors believe that it is very difficult for the average diet to supply all of the essential nutrients needed by a pregnant or postpartum woman. Dr. Judith Moore, a doctor of osteopathic medicine in Provo, Utah, recommends the following vitamin and mineral supplements to help mothers suffering from postpartum depression:

1. *A daily multivitamin/mineral supplement*—to ensure that minimum Recommended Daily Allowance (RDA) levels of nutrients are met.
2. *800 mg of calcium per day in chelated form, preferably one that also contains trace minerals and Vitamin D*—to ensure proper bones, muscle, and nerve function and to help calm the system.
3. *200 to 800 mg of magnesium per day in chelated form, along with potassium, and sodium*—to help with hormonal imbalances, cramps, and many other health risks for women.
4. *Vitamin B complex*—to maintain proper neurotransmitter function.
5. *Omega-3 and omega-6 fatty acids*—for proper brain and nerve function,
6. *Trace minerals*—including minerals such as zinc, selenium, and chromium, which have antioxidant and other benefits.

Vitamins alone, in most cases, will not resolve serious depression symptoms, but they may help speed the recovery process.

Marie Osmond, Marcia Wilkie, and Judith Moore, *Behind the Smile: My Journey Out of Postpartum Depression*, New York: Warner Books, Inc., 2001, p. 288.

that contains folate, and then prescribe additional folate supplements, along with vitamins B6 and B12, if blood tests suggest that more is needed. Omega-3 fatty acids are another essential nutrient sometimes found lacking in depressed patients. Omega-3 fatty acids, along with omega-6 fatty acids, are critical to the proper functioning of brain chemicals, particularly serotonin and dopamine. Although typical American diets tend to be high in omega-6 fatty acids (found in vegetable oils such as corn and soybean oils), they are often deficient in omega-3 fatty acids (found in fish such as tuna and salmon). Some nutritionists believe eating foods rich in omega-3 fatty acids or taking omega-3 supplements may help to support brain chemistry and combat symptoms of depression.

Various other nutrients are similarly involved in the production of brain chemicals and may be potentially helpful in treating depression. For example, 5-Hydroxytryptophan (5-HTP) is a by-product of tryptophan, an amino acid necessary for the body's production of serotonin. Some alternative medicine supporters think 5-HTP could prove to be as effective as SSRIs and other antidepressants in treating depression, but with fewer side effects. Further research is needed, however, because this nutrient has on rare occasions been linked with a condition known as eosinophilic myalgia syndrome (EMS), a potentially fatal disorder that affects the skin, blood, muscles, and organs. Other nutritional aids that may prove useful in combating depression include selenium (a mineral found in wheat germ, brewer's yeast, liver, fish, shellfish, garlic, sunflower seeds, Brazil nuts, and grains), inositol (a substance considered part of the vitamin B complex found in cereals, nuts, beans, and fruits), and melatonin (a hormone produced by the brain's pineal gland).

Acupuncture and Other Alternative Therapies

A variety of other alternative medicine therapies also have their supporters. Acupuncture, for example, is a traditional Chinese medical practice that has become popular in treating a number

Light therapy uses between 7,000 and 10,000 lux (a unit of intensity) of light to lift depression.

of disorders. It works by inserting tiny needles at particular points in the body believed to be meridians for "chi," a Chinese word meaning life energy. Studies have shown that acupuncture, by stimulating nerves in skin and muscles and helping to release natural painkillers such as endorphin and serotonin, can relieve chronic anxiety and depression.

Another promising alternative technique is light therapy, which uses between 7,000 and 10,000 lux (a unit of intensity) of light to lift depression. No one is sure exactly how this works, but it may somehow reduce the brain's production of melatonin, which can cause drowsiness and fatigue. Studies conducted on pregnant women in 2002 and 2004 showed that light therapy can have dramatic effects, in some cases even producing a complete remission of major depression symptoms. Many PPD experts are very encouraged by these results. Misri writes,

Nondrug Therapies

Bright-light therapy is an appealing and—based on the research—apparently viable form of therapy for pregnant women and postpartum breast-feeding women who are reluctant to expose their babies to medications. It's easy to use, available at home, and doesn't require women to travel to therapy sessions.[20]

Some women have tried homeopathy, a 200-year-old system designed to stimulate the body's own natural defense mechanisms by treating patients with greatly diluted solutions of plant extracts. This type of treatment is often recommended by naturopaths, health practitioners who use natural methods rather than drugs or surgery to treat disease. However, homeopathy is not always effective and has not been widely studied for use with postpartum patients.

Massage and other types of body work can also be quite useful to those battling depression. Many massage therapists and other body-work practitioners believe that emotions can be

Massage can be a relaxing and pleasurable way to relieve stress and depression.

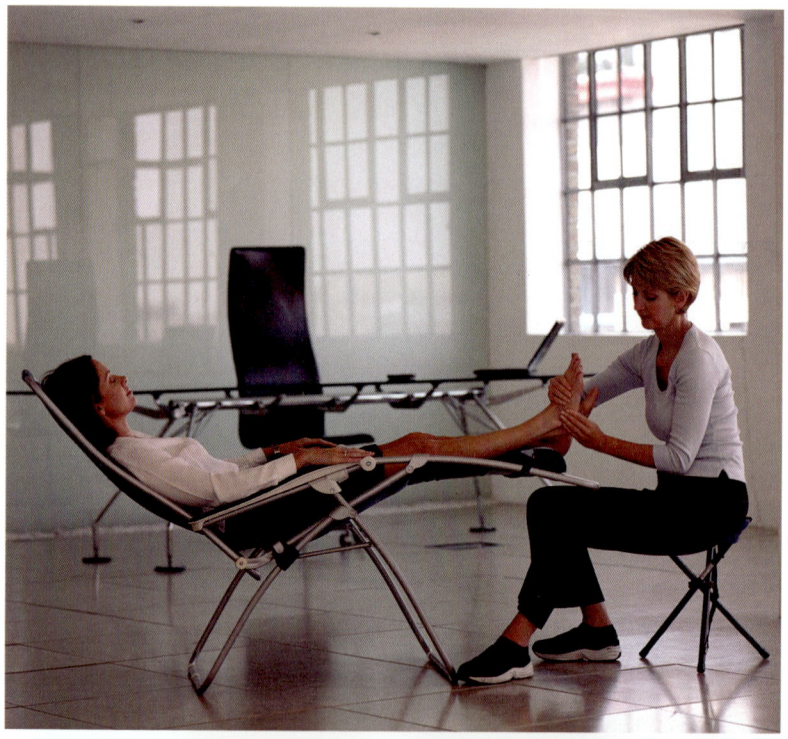

There are many alternative treatments, such as reflexology, aromatherapy, and hypnosis that can help relieve symptoms of depression.

stored in the body's muscles and tissues, so it may be possible for a woman's negative emotions to be released by having her body worked on. At the very least, massage can help patients to relax and let go of stress.

Still other women choose alternative treatments such as reflexology, which involves massaging reflex points on the hands or feet to stimulate the nervous system, or aromatherapy, the use of essential oils and plant essences to stimulate the immune system and encourage healing. Hypnosis, a method of putting patients into a trance-like state to help them change behaviors, has been shown to be helpful for many people who want to stop addictions, compulsions, or phobias, which are often an aspect of postpartum depression. However, hypnosis is not believed to have any significant effect on the depression itself.

Although these alternative strategies may not completely solve PPD on their own, they may be of great benefit in combination with other types of treatment. In fact, a growing number of medical doctors encourage the use of alternative strategies to complement their medical plan of action. As psychiatry professor and PPD expert Victoria Hendrick explains, "Many alternative treatments have the advantages of being inexpensive, accessible, and generally safe and well-tolerated, thereby presenting attractive options to traditional treatments for postpartum depression."[21]

On the other hand, these alternative therapies are not regulated by the government to ensure they meet objective standards of care, and there is a lack of scientific evidence to show their effectiveness in treating PPD. Experts say it is important, therefore, for women to coordinate with their primary doctors and psychotherapists before adding alternative therapies or substituting them for more conventional medical or psychological treatments.

Self-Help Strategies

With such a wide assortment of medical, psychological, and alternative treatment options available, however, a woman's

Self-nurturing behaviors can help women overcome PPD.

most difficult task may be deciding which one or ones she should choose to treat her PPD symptoms. Making such a complex decision would be difficult under any circumstances, but it is even harder for women who are severely depressed, anxious, and not thinking clearly. Although taking action seems daunting, experts urge women in this position to force themselves to reach out to others, such as their primary care doctor or a therapist, and ask for guidance in weighing the pros and cons of various treatment options.

Regardless of what treatment a woman chooses to deal with her depression, she will always benefit from self-nurturing behaviors. Although there is a strong tendency on the part of new mothers to focus only on the new baby's needs, it is equally important for her to take care of herself as well. In fact,

Nondrug Therapies

ensuring her own health and happiness is the best gift a new mother can give to her infant. What this means can vary from person to person, but for many, self-care can include prayer and participation in religious or spiritual rituals, transcendental meditation, yoga, getting enough sleep, and focusing on good nutrition. For some it might mean resisting the temptation to self-medicate with toxic substances such as cigarettes, alcohol, marijuana, or other illegal drugs. Self-nurturing also can be as simple as telephoning or seeing close friends, getting out of the house for walks, or even playing with a pet. Certain activities, like listening to music, exercising, and doing anything one loves to do, have actually been found to increase endorphin levels and improve mood.

All of these actions help to lessen the stress of being a new mother and contribute to good mental and physical health. Although most women with postpartum depression will also need some type of counseling, these self-help strategies can complement psychotherapy as well as any other alternative, non-drug treatments they may choose.

CHAPTER FOUR

Effects of PPD on the Child and Others

A postpartum woman's struggle with depression is made even more difficult because it affects not only her, but those around her. If not treated, a mother's feelings of sadness and anxiety can prevent her from providing the important emotional bonding critical for all newborns. On the other hand, if the mother pursues treatment and wants to breast-feed, she must navigate a minefield of information about what effects conventional or alternative medications might have on her baby. Of course, depression can also put great strain on husbands and

Depression in a new mother can strain relationships with her partner and family.

other family members, affecting marriages and other important relationships.

The Effect of Medications on the Child

Perhaps the biggest concern for a mother suffering from depression is how recommended PPD medications will affect her baby if she continues to breast-feed. The vast majority of new mothers in the United States want to breast-feed their infants because of the many benefits offered by breast milk. Misri notes that "Breast milk is healthy from a nutritional point of view; it is believed to protect the baby from certain illnesses; it's cheap; and in most cases it's readily available."[22] For these reasons, breast-feeding is encouraged in the United States by the American Academy of Pediatrics and promoted throughout the world by the World Health Organization. Women sometimes feel pressured to breast-feed by the expectations of friends and family members. For PPD mothers who feel they need medication to treat their depression, therefore, the choices are either to take the medication and stop breast-feeding or to continue breast-feeding and expose their babies to antidepressant drugs.

Fortunately, according to most experts, the good news is that although all medications are secreted into breast milk, the amounts reaching infants are tiny and many medications prescribed for symptoms of PPD appear to be safe for the child. In fact, most doctors now encourage PPD mothers to continue breast-feeding because of the known benefits for the baby, and because extensive research on antidepressants has failed to suggest major or widespread risks. As psychiatrist and Emory University professor Zachary Stowe explains,

> We know more about antidepressants and breast milk than we know about any other class of medication in the world.... We have studied them extensively because we were afraid of them, but we have not found any pattern of consistent adverse problems associated with antidepressant use and breast-feeding.[23]

PPD can affect all members in the family.

SSRI antidepressants, the most commonly prescribed type of medication for postpartum depression, appear to be particularly safe for nursing mothers and their babies. In studies of SSRI medications such as Prozac, Paxil, and Zoloft, for example, the vast majority of babies exposed to the drugs showed absolutely no adverse reactions, and the few babies who did seem to react exhibited only minor behavioral symptoms such as colic and hyperactivity. More research needs to be done on other SSRI drugs, such as Celexa, as well as on SNRI drugs such as Effexor, but so far these medications have also produced no reported problems.

However, a number of other PPD medications do appear to present health risks for breast-fed babies. Doctors generally advise women not to breast-feed while taking Lithium, for example, because of its highly toxic effects on the heart. There

Effects of PPD on the Child and Others

is also concern about other mood stabilizer medications used for bipolar conditions, including Depakote (valproic acid), Tegretol (carbamazepine), Lamictal (lamotrigine), Neurontin (gabapentin), and Topamax (topiramate). These drugs have not been sufficiently studied to determine their toxicity to infants and some of them have been reported to cause problems for some babies. Information is also lacking on many of the antipsychotic drugs, and benzodiazepines are not recommended for breast-feeding women because of their relatively long effects and risks of dependency.

If a woman does choose to medicate during breast-feeding, there are ways to minimize the baby's exposure to depression medications. For example, many SSRI medications tend to be concentrated in the higher-fat milk (called hindmilk) that the baby sucks at the end of a feeding, so mothers can feed more often and for shorter periods to reduce the amount of hindmilk given to the baby. In addition, various medications peak in the breast milk at different times, and knowing this can help a mother determine when to breast-feed. For example, Zoloft peaks in breast milk about eight to nine hours after it is taken by the mother, so she could reduce her baby's exposure by pumping and discarding her milk at that time of day. Alternately, she could nurse her baby and then take the medication afterwards. Finally, mothers can choose medications that have the lowest risk for their babies. An analysis of fifty-seven studies of antidepressant drugs recently showed, for example, that among the SSRIs, Paxil and Zoloft are the preferred medications for breast-feeding women because they were virtually undetectable in the infants' blood samples. Prozac, on the other hand, produced the highest levels in babies' blood tests, despite resulting in serious adverse effects.

Babies can also be monitored during the mother's treatment period, either by measuring the amount of medication in the mother's blood and breast milk or, if available, by the use of sophisticated blood tests that can measure minute levels of the prescribed medications in the babies' blood. Even without testing, however, mothers often can recognize if their babies are exhibiting unusual symptoms, such as excessive drowsiness, irritability, or fussiness. If tests suggest the baby may be affected, or if the mother becomes uncomfortable with the idea of taking medication while nursing, experts say it is important that she does not suddenly stop or lower her dosage of medication. Depending on the medication, such a decision might cause a relapse of depression or other problems. It is better for a woman to work with her doctor to gradually wean herself and her baby away from the PPD drug.

Effects of Alternative Treatments on the Child

Despite the assurances from doctors that many medications are safe, however, some mothers are wary of exposing their infants to any type of drug during the time they are breast-feeding. For those mothers who feel strongly about this, the choice is often to forgo all pharmaceutical medications in favor of one or more of the alternative therapies available to them. Some of these therapies, such as massage, light therapy, and some vitamins, appear to be completely safe, creating absolutely no risks for the breast-feeding child. Many other alternative treatments for depression, however, have not been studied for their effects on breast milk and for this reason are often not recommended.

The experts are divided, for example, on whether St. John's Wort should be taken while breast-feeding. One 2002 study found that levels of the herb found in breast milk ranged between low to below detection limits, with no side effects to either mothers or babies, but still more research needs to be done. In light of these unknowns, many experts warn against taking St. John's Wort while breast-feeding, or they suggest that mother and child at least be monitored for potential side effects and be under a doctor's care.

Ruth A. Lawrence, professor of Pediatrics, Obstetrics & Gynecology at the University of Rochester School of Medicine & Dentistry explains:

> Breast-feeding mothers should not take St. John's Wort

without consulting their physician first. Although it is a natural substance, St. John's Wort works like many other antidepressants and can be dangerous if not used appropriately. It can reduce the effect of some prescription drugs, for example, and should not be taken with other antidepressants. . . . The combination of St. John's Wort and ragweed exposure can cause a very serious allergic reaction in individuals who have allergies, especially asthma. The herb also can cause skin burns in light-skinned people because is contains hypersen, a photosensitizing substance that reacts with light. Even though a prescription is not required, it is wise to talk with your physician before taking St. John's Wort regularly.[24]

Effects of Non-Treatment on the Child

Other mothers simply choose not to pursue any type of treatment during the postpartum period if they want to breast-feed their children. Yet if depression is not treated, either during or after pregnancy, it can cause significant harm to the child that may be equal to or more than the risks associated with medication.

The most damaging effect of non-treatment is that depressed mothers often fail to bond with or interact frequently with their babies. Depression may also cause mothers to be irritable, impatient, and low energy—all symptoms that may, in turn, limit their ability to be good mothers to their children. Research suggests, for example, that maternal depression tends to produce negative parenting behaviors, such as yelling and spanking, and low levels of positive parenting behaviors, such as reading or playing with the child.

These behaviors can produce significant problems for the child later in life. PPD experts Margaret L. Moline, David A. Kahn, Ruth W. Ross, Lori L. Altshuler, and Lee S. Cohen have noted that "Such children may not perform as well on some developmental tasks as children of mothers who were not depressed. Their ability to interact with other children may also be affected, and they may have behavioral and learning problems."[25] Studies also show that children of depressed mothers often suffer from hyperactivity, language problems, lower weights, and even higher rates of hypertension and disease later in life. The worst case scenario, of course, is the case of the untreated bipolar mother who lapses into psychosis and causes harm to, or even kills, her child.

All of these risks, experts say, are good reasons for mothers to seek help and treatment for their PPD symptoms, if only for the good of the child. Women adamant about not exposing their babies to medications instead of avoiding treatment could potentially stop breast-feeding after the first couple of weeks of the postpartum period so that they can take antidepressant medications. At the very least, experts say, women can seek psychological help to help them cope with their depression symptoms so that they can properly take care of their newborns. In the end, however, experts and doctors can only give their advice; the treatment decision is a personal one that only the PPD mother can make.

Postpartum Depression and Fathers

A new mother's depression also has a significant effect on others in the family besides the newborn, most particularly the baby's father. Many fathers, for example, identify closely with their wives during and immediately after pregnancy. Some expectant fathers even experience symptoms of pregnancy similar to those reported by their partners, such as food cravings, weight gain, morning sickness, or cramps. This tendency for dads to sympathize with their pregnant wives is called Couvade syndrome, from the French word *couver*, which means "to incubate." In fact, studies that examined the hormone levels in expectant men's blood and saliva found hormonal shifts similar to those of pregnant women, including, for example, a reduction of the male hormone testosterone immediately after birth. It seems clear, therefore, that men, like women, often approach childbirth and parenthood with a certain amount of stress and anxiety.

A Father's Thoughts

The following is an excerpt from a father's account of his reaction to his wife's postpartum depression:

John.... I don't want to do this anymore."... "Do what?"... "Keep living". That was my introduction to the world of Post-Partum Depression (PPD). Like most people I had heard about PPD, but I had no idea how serious it was. I certainly never thought that my wife [Pam] would ever lose hope to the point that she wanted to end her life. I also had no idea how to get help. Nothing in my life has come close to causing as much worry, anger, frustration, despair, and fear as dealing with PPD. For us, PPD came on very unexpectedly. After our daughter [Jodi] was born it seemed like everything was going great.... Then things started to change.... At some point the normal concern that a mother has for her baby turned into a dark cloud that consumed Pam. She was unable to sleep and became almost obsessed with the baby's eating habits.... We called our pediatrician and got a recommendation for a psychiatrist [who prescribed various medications].... I credit them with saving her life.

Postpartum Dads, "John's Story," undated. https://home.comcast.net/~ddklinker/mysite2/Johns_Story.htm.

If this natural pre-childbirth anxiety is heightened by the onset of symptoms of serious depression or anxiety in the mother during the postpartum period, fathers can quickly become similarly overwhelmed with worries and fears. Indeed, researchers have found that a mother's postpartum depression significantly affects the mood of the father. A study published in 2006, for example, found that almost as many new fathers (10 percent) as mothers (14 percent) suffer moderate to severe depression after the birth of a child. As men, they want to fix their wives' problems logically, but they often find that no matter what they do for their partner, it isn't enough. Their frustration at not being able to solve the PPD problem is further exacerbated frequently by the loss of intimacy with their partners. After childbirth, a woman often has little interest in sex and wants to focus only on her baby, and this disinterest in her husband is multiplied if a woman feels depressed or anxious about motherhood. The couple's ability to be mutually supportive and intimate may be further damaged if the couple disagrees and argues about how best to parent the baby. The result for fathers, in many cases, is that they feel left out of the mother-child relationship as well as angry that their own needs are not being met.

On top of these problems, if the mother becomes completely dysfunctional as a result of severe PPD, fathers may have to become the primary caregivers for the new baby as well as the main breadwinner for the family—a heavy burden that further increases male anxiety. Men, therefore, may become as depressed as their partners during the postpartum period. Misri writes, "Fathers, too, can suffer postpartum depression. Particularly if a man has a family history of depression, this is a time of vulnerability for him, just as it is for a woman."[26]

And if both parents are struggling with depression or anxiety, the chances that the infant will be affected rise significantly. Just like PPD mothers, fathers suffering from depression tend to interact less frequently with their babies, leading to impairment of the father-child relationship. Researchers at the Center for Pediatric Research at the Eastern Virginia Medical School in Norfolk, Virginia, for example, found that.

> Where day-to-day interactions are concerned, depressed . . . fathers engage in less positive interaction with their children, with a particular reduction in the degree of enrichment interactions, including reading, telling stories, and singing songs."[27]

Effects of PPD on the Child and Others

Neglect of the baby by both the father and the mother greatly increases the risk of harm to babies. A recent study of thousands of parents and children covering the three years following childbirth, for example, found that the risk of behavioral problems in children doubled when both mothers and fathers were depressed at a point about eight weeks after the birth.

In situations of couples depression, the entire family relationship can even be put into serious jeopardy, and PPD can become an underlying factor in serious marital friction and divorce. The answer, experts say, is for both members of the couple to seek professional help. Shari I. Lusskin, director of reproductive psychiatry at NYU School of Medicine, explains that

> Depression is a medical condition, not a moral condition.... If you feel that your mood is not what it should be after the birth of a child, or if you feel your partner's mood is abnormal, seek help and seek help early. The sooner you get treated, the better—and the fewer consequences for the mother, the father, and the child.[28]

In many cases, however, depression in fathers may be even more hidden and denied than when it afflicts mothers. Whereas women with depression tend to show clear signs of sadness, men struggling with depression are more likely to act irritably and to withdraw. William Coleman, professor of pediatrics at the University of North Carolina and chairman of the American Academy of Pediatrics, explains, "[A depressed father simply] tends to work longer, to watch sports more, to drink more and be solitary."[29] Some experts say that pediatricians should make a better effort to identify depression in both mothers and fathers, since they are often in the best position to learn about family dynamics following childbirth.

Postpartum Depression and Other Family Members

Post-childbirth depression can also affect other members of the family. Indeed, many experts argue that PPD is really a family

A Difficult Legal Defense

Postpartum depression is recognized as a legal defense in many countries, but it is especially difficult to prove under U.S. law. Many countries, such as Great Britain, have infanticide laws that allow a woman with postpartum depression who kills a child under the age of one to escape a charge of murder. Under these laws, such a mother would only be charged with manslaughter, and most likely be sentenced to probation instead of jail time, if she can prove that she was mentally ill for reasons related to giving birth. In the United States, however, mothers who kill their children can only use postpartum depression as part of an insanity defense, a much higher standard. If the defense is successful, the jury can find the defendant not guilty by reason of insanity, but in many states, she would be committed to a psychiatric facility. On the other hand, if she is found guilty of murder, the mother can present evidence of her mental condition as a mitigating factor for the jury to consider during the sentencing phase of the trial, a tactic that might save her from the death penalty but still get her life in prison.

problem. Paul Ramchandani, a consultant in child and adolescent psychiatry at the United Kingdom's University of Oxford, writes that "At the time of childbirth we focus on mothers. But actually we should be paying attention to the wider family. The birth of a child is a fantastic thing, but it is also a time of intense change, and that impacts the whole family."[30]

If a mother is coping with depression or anxiety and struggling to take care of a newborn at the same time, for example, not only is her interest in and ability to take care of the new baby compromised, but also her ability to care for any of her other children. Likewise, the father's stress in such a situation only adds to the children's problems. If prolonged, this paren-

Effects of PPD on the Child and Others

tal neglect can cause emotional damage that can reverberate within the family far into the future.

Depression in the family following childbirth can also affect relationships with members of the extended family. Grandparents and other family members generally expect that the birth of a child will bring joy to the family, not pain, so the onset of PPD can cause hurt feelings and disruptions in families that could be easily misunderstood. These family repercussions, experts say, underscore the need for a mother with PPD symptoms to seek help and for family members to be taught to understand the disease of PPD so that they can be supportive instead of offended.

In fact, PPD experts stress that grandparents, other members of the extended family, and close friends can provide desperately needed help for a new mother suffering from depression. PPD organizations suggest, for example, that grandparents and others try to be receptive listeners, understand the depressed mother's need to cry, and encourage her to talk to a health professional. Extended family members and friends can also be of invaluable help to new mothers by offering to provide meals, run errands, do laundry and housework, or babysit. Most importantly, friends and family must avoid criticism, denial, or rejection. With patience and support from those who love her, a mother suffering from PPD has a much better chance of finding her way out of the darkness of depression.

CHAPTER FIVE

The Road to Recovery

Once a woman suffering from PPD manages to reach out for treatment, the recovery process can take many months and be very difficult. For many women, even after a clear diagnosis, it is hard to accept the idea that they are depressed to such an extent that they cannot solve the problem on their own. Other patients fail to follow the prescribed treatment plan for a variety of reasons or lose hope when treatment does not result in an immediate fix. If patients can stay committed to the treatment process, however, PPD is usually a temporary illness from which patients do recover.

Following the Treatment Plan

Even after they have been diagnosed with PPD, many women resist treatment for some of the same reasons that they resist reporting their symptoms in the first place. They may continue to live in denial of the idea that they really have clinical depression or that they need treatment, hoping that their doctors have made a mistake. Or they may just find it hard to accept that their dream of a perfect pregnancy and delivery and a happy relationship with their baby has not come true. This is particularly true for women who, before their pregnancies, were very independent, self-reliant, and successful in business or other work. PPD experts Ronald Rosenberg, Deborah Greening, and James Windell explain, "While there's something admirable about self-reliance and while being fiercely independent can be a strength in the business world or the arts, it can play havoc

The Road to Recovery

with you when you have postpartum depression and need to ask for help."[31]

Some women, too, may have disapproving and unsupportive family members or friends who continue to deny there is a problem. Out of concerns for the baby, these people may even openly criticize the new mother for taking medication or pursuing other types of treatment. Such sabotage can even come from total strangers. In 2005, this negative dynamic splashed onto the pages of national celebrity magazines and television shows when actor Tom Cruise publicly criticized actress Brooke Shields for taking an antidepressant medication for PPD after the birth of her first child. Cruise claimed that antidepressants are dangerous and recommended that women with postpartum depression instead pursue vitamin treatment. Shields responded, "Tom Cruise's comments are irresponsible and dangerous. Tom should . . . let women who are experiencing postpartum depression decide what treatment options are best for them."[32]

Of course, there is also the problem of navigating the highly complex and sometimes frustrating U.S. health care system. Although there are numerous highly qualified and caring health professionals, many are extremely busy and some are not well-versed in the proper treatment of PPD. Finding the right doctor may take time as well as persistence—a reality that may be very discouraging to a woman who is severely depressed. And once a sensitive and effective doctor is found, a patient may still face problems with health care and disability insurance providers, some of whom may be more interested in saving their company money than in providing adequate health services to postpartum women in great need. Experts say it is all too common for insurers to challenge doctors' diagnoses, recommendations for treatment, or assessments of disability. For these reasons, finding health care providers willing to fight the health care system on the patient's behalf may be critical to a woman's recovery from PPD.

Other obstacles to treatment may include financial and work stresses. The expense of paying for the portion of medical care not covered by health insurance or trying alternative treatments not eligible for insurance coverage may come at a time when the family is already experiencing money problems due to the costs of the pregnancy and delivery. Financial difficulties or pressure from employers may also cause the new mother to return to work more quickly than the treatment plan would recommend. And once she returns to work, she may be reluctant to take time off from work to attend psychotherapy or other doctors' appointments. Indeed, it is usually difficult enough for new mothers to juggle all the normal demands of motherhood, marriage, and household duties, along with full- or part-time paid work, without having to find extra time and energy to squeeze in treatment commitments.

Working With Doctors

Women who are depressed also often fail to follow treatment advice simply because they are depressed and not thinking clearly. In fact, research has found that patients in general tend to ignore their doctors' advice. University of California at Riverside psychology professor Robin DiMatteo writes that "The problem of noncompliance is quite large. . . . Overall, about 40 percent of people leave their doctors' offices and do not follow recommendations."[33] Depression only increases the likelihood that a patient will ignore or make mistakes in implementing the recommendations of the treatment plan.

Experts stress, however, that it is extremely important for PPD mothers to make every effort to carefully follow treatment advice and make changes only with the help of their physicians. If the patient is honest with her caregivers—making sure to reveal crucial details about whether she is taking medications as directed, how she is feeling, and how she is reacting to medications and therapies—doctors and other health care workers can do a much better job of prescribing the most effective and appropriate remedies to cure her depression. Keeping a daily diary may help a depressed mother to remember and keep track of information that may be useful to her doctors or therapists. Hiding information, on the other hand, only slows recovery. Above all, experts say it is important for PPD mothers to visit their doctors and other health caregivers regularly for check-ups during the recovery period so that they have the opportunity to monitor medications frequently and make the adjustments that may be necessary or helpful to speed up recovery.

Adopting Positive Behaviors

A woman's rate of recovery from PPD will also depend, in large part, on whether she actively cultivates positive attitudes and behaviors that contribute to her health and well-being. For many women, this begins with accepting the fact that life has changed with motherhood. Being a good mother may mean acclimating to major lifestyle changes while learning a completely new job that has many stresses, mundane chores, and long hours. Dr. Sandra L. Wheatley explains,

> The simple reality of motherhood is that it isn't glamorous, it isn't well paid, it is often dreadfully repetitive, it is often carried out on your own, and it can be very stressful. Of course it does have wonderful heart-stopping, stomach-flipping, face-splitting ecstatic times too. So, it is important to have a balanced image of motherhood, and that includes both positive and negative."[34]

Accepting the reality of depressive illness during this postpartum period requires even more patience and may mean giving up ideas of perfection and control that have formed part of a woman's core identity before becoming pregnant. Experts advise new mothers to consciously let go of self-berating thoughts and feelings, reduce their expectations of being a perfect mother, and try to substitute accepting and positive thoughts in their place. This involves blocking negative thoughts when daily disasters strike, such as when the baby won't stop crying, fails to sleep, or has trouble nursing. Or it may mean the mother must forgive herself for those instances when she feels too tired or depressed to do more than take care of her baby's physical

Support groups help those who suffer from PPD share with others who may be going through the same difficulties.

needs. Accepting that life is tough at the moment and not blaming herself or others for her depression is essential to forward progress during the treatment of depression.

Accepting PPD may also require the mother to take better care of herself during the recovery period by making sure to get enough rest, make time for exercise, and maintain a healthy diet and lifestyle. Experts say it is also important for new mothers to take some personal time for themselves so they don't become resentful of their babies or others around them. Making time each day to do at least one small thing that makes them feel better—whether it is taking a hot bath, getting a manicure, reading a magazine, taking a walk, watching a TV program, or calling a friend—can be a tremendous help to move depressed women into a healthier and less depressed mindset.

The Road to Recovery

Perhaps the most important thing a PPD mother can do to foster her recovery, however, is to ask for and accept help from others. As PPD experts Ronald Rosenberg, Deborah Greening, and James Windell put it, "No matter how courageous and self-reliant you are, if you have postpartum depression, you will need the ongoing support of others in order to recover."[35] Support from a husband or partner in the home is invaluable and can often be the determining factor during a patient's recovery from PPD. As the person who is most intimate with the new mother and baby, the husband not only can provide daily emotional reassurance and support; he also can be a great help with the practical needs of the family and can make sure the mother gets enough food and rest and is complying with the requirements of her treatment plan. Dr. Sandra L. Wheatley, for example, suggests that a father try to reassure the depressed mother that she will get well, tell her that he loves her and cuddle her often throughout every day, and praise her by pointing out small improvements in her behavior and attitude. He also can help her to eat properly by helping to keep groceries in the house and ensure that she gets as much sleep as possible by helping to soothe or feed the baby at night. Other suggestions include encouraging the new mom to be active and exercise, giving her a massage, and arranging for a babysitter so that they can go out together as a couple.

Although other family members and friends are often not living in the home, they can be a great help during the postpartum period. Simply asking what they can do to help the depressed mother may work as a first step, because once she thinks about it, she can probably suggest what would make her feel better. Important roles for family and friends in the support network include offering continuing encouragement, supporting her choice of treatment, and providing practical help with child care, shopping, washing, cleaning, and other chores. Sometimes just providing a patient, nonjudgmental, listening ear and allowing the depressed mother to talk about her feelings and problems is the most appreciated gift of support. Just knowing that people love her and are concerned about her can give a

Advice for Fathers

Fathers are often the first to notice when their partners become anxious or depressed following childbirth. Some of the most important tips for the partners of women suffering from postpartum depression include:

1. *Seek information and help.* Fathers must educate themselves so they understand that postpartum depression is treatable and so they can talk about it with their doctors.
2. *Find an expert.* It is important to get a referral to a psychiatrist, psychologist, or a physician trained in the area of postpartum depression.
3. *Seek emergency treatment if necessary.* Take the mother to the nearest emergency room and have her admitted if there is any danger that she may harm herself or the child.
4. *Get support from family and friends.* Do not hesitate to ask for help from others during this tough period.
5. *Be patient.* The treatment process may be slow and it may take months for mothers to fully recover.
6. *Be supportive.* Try not to minimize symptoms or become angry with the mother. This is a time when she desperately needs your love and support.
7. *Maintain hope.* Your partner will recover, and life will return to normal in time.

PPD mother the strength and will to stick with her treatment plan and overcome her feelings of depression. Support groups, too, can be useful by providing the depressed mother with the chance to discuss the ups and downs of recovery with others who share her feelings and problems.

Becoming a Confident Parent

Many experts also believe in the power of parent support and training groups during the recovery period both to help depressed mothers develop confidence in their mothering abilities and to minimize the effects of the mother's depression on the child. This training can take several forms. One type of parenting training, for example, teaches and encourages mothers to talk, smile, play, and interact more with the baby in order to establish closeness between mother and child. Group lead-

The Value of Support

Connecting with others and getting their support can be an essential lifeline for those afflicted with postpartum depression. The following blog from writer Katherine Stone on her Web site *Postpartum Progress* describes the terrible feeling of isolation she felt during her postpartum struggle:

> When you suffer from a postpartum mood disorder, you walk around in a haze while trying to seem as normal as possible. You try to make yourself feel as connected as you can to your child and those around you. Perhaps your dearest friends and family can tell that you don't seem like yourself, but then they just brush it off as normal baby blues. And you soldier on, trying to pretend—sometimes successfully, sometimes not so successfully—that everything is cool.... One of the truly awful feelings you experience during postpartum mood disorders is that sense of disconnection from the world, from your friends and family, from your baby, and most of all, from yourself. I felt so deeply, deeply alone. Profoundly alone.

Katherine Stone, "Profoundly Alone: The Disconnection of Postpartum Depression," February 12, 2007. http://postpartumprogress.typepad.com/weblog/2007/02/profoundly_alon.html.

ers model these behaviors for mothers to show them how to use expressive language and other tools to stimulate the baby. For example, mothers are encouraged to talk to the baby as much as possible, smile and laugh often, make faces, sing to the baby, or dance with him or her. Other suggestions are to read to the baby, play with toys, or make a game out of simple chores such as changing diapers. Virtually any kind of safe, positive interaction, experts say, will teach the child important social and motor skills, strengthen the mother-child bond, and at the same time help the mother to banish her depression.

Massaging the infant is another tool often used in parent training. Like language and social interaction, touch helps to develop a close bond between mother and child while also helping the mother feel better. It also has the added benefit of reducing stress for the baby. Babies who are fussy, teething, or having difficulty sleeping are often comforted by massage, and this in turn, reduces stress for the mothers.

Finally, parent training can teach new parents how to set appropriate limits and handle discipline with babies who are learning important socialization skills. Dealing with toddlers who are in the "terrible twos" (roughly the period when children are between 12 and 36 months old) can be especially trying and frustrating for any parent, and even more so for a mother who is depressed. Learning ways to avoid excessive punishment and redirect children into appropriate behaviors can help reduce the stress of this period for PPD mothers and their partners.

A Slow Recovery from Postpartum Depression

If a depressed mother is given appropriate treatment and support and as she acquires greater confidence in her parenting abilities, she should begin to see improvement in her depressive symptoms. Even in the best of circumstances, however, experts warn that recovery from an illness like PPD is gradual and full of ups and downs. As with any illness, therefore, patients should not expect instant recovery but must learn to accept small improvements that will eventually lead them out of PPD

The Road to Recovery

in a period of, on average, four to twelve months. PPD expert Sandra Wheatley suggests that mothers

> Try to take life one day at a time. There will be good days and there will be bad days. Slowly but surely, once you have found and accepted practical help and emotional support that suits you, you will notice that the good days start to outnumber the bad days. . . . A gradual return to wellness is not just what is likely to happen, it is also advisable. Imagine you had broken your leg. On the day you had the plaster taken off you would not expect to be able to walk around on it as if it had never been broken. The same is true with your mind.[36]

For some women, however, recovery can take years. For Judy Swartley, an accomplished woman with master's degrees in industrial engineering and business and a job as a management consultant, it took a full five years. Swartley, who describes herself as a "ball of energy, a real 'in-control' type of person—someone who had a sense of power that I could accomplish anything I wanted," felt the classic symptoms of PPD just days after the birth of her child. She explains, "I had no desire to eat, to hold my baby—no desire for anything."[37] After seeing several doctors who failed to help her, Swartley found a psychiatrist who immediately diagnosed PPD and prescribed anti-depressants and psychotherapy. Swartley says she was able to eat and sleep again within three days of starting the medication, but it took her five long years to get back to normal, and her recovery period was characterized by unpredictable swings of forward progress and backward regression. Swartley says, "I will never forget how horrible it was to go through . . . . I would never want to see someone who could be helped go through what I did."[38]

Signs of Recovery

Perhaps the clearest sign of recovery, experts say, is when a mother starts to regain a feeling of control that was lost when she first became powerless over her depression. Studies by C.T. Beck, a nurse researcher and certified nurse midwife, for example, have identified a four-stage process of recovery from PPD: (1) encountering terror; (2) dying of self; (3) struggling to survive; and (4) regaining control.

The first stage, encountering terror, comes when a new mother first begins feeling the symptoms of PPD, such as anxiety, sadness, or foggy thinking. During stage two, dying of self, many women disconnect from their partners and the world, becoming socially isolated. Some women, at this point, entertain thoughts of death, suicide, or harming their babies, thoughts that fuel feelings of shame and low self-worth. The third stage, struggling to survive, occurs when women realize they must get help. Typical coping strategies during this period include praying for relief, visiting health care providers, or searching out a PPD support group. Often, the effort to find treatment is met with disappointment, when doctors or others minimize women's concerns, requiring them to battle the system to obtain appropriate care.

The final stage is recovery, which Beck calls regaining control, when the mother begins the difficult process of reclaiming her life. Beck describes this period as one of unpredictable transitioning, mourning lost time, and guarded recovering. Moving out of PPD is unpredictable because it is erratic, with some normal days and others when the woman still feels horribly depressed. As this process continues, many women also realize that their depression has caused them to lose time with their infants, leaving them feeling cheated or even sadder. Finally, women reach a time of guarded recovery, when they are feeling much better most of the time. Despite the improvement in their mental health, however, most women who have experienced PPD are left feeling vulnerable, with the knowledge that if it happened once, depression could one day return.

Maintaining Hope

The key throughout the recovery period, experts say, is for the depressed postpartum mother and those who love her to main-

The Road to Recovery

tain hope. It is vitally important for the patient, her husband, her family, her friends, and all concerned to remember that PPD is a temporary illness and that there is a positive future ahead. Judith Moore, a doctor that singer Marie Osmond consulted when she was experiencing PPD, writes:

> Postpartum depression is a treatable condition. Help is available.... You are not alone. Thousands of women are experiencing the same feelings you are. By finding and treating the physical and emotional causes of PPD, each mother can learn to find again the joy that life has to offer.[39]

Singer Marie Osmond wrote a book about her experience with PPD.

Notes

Introduction: When Motherhood Becomes a Nightmare

1. Quoted in Carol Smith, "Severe Postpartum Depression Leaves Them Without Wife and Mother," *Seattle Post-Intellgencer*, January 16, 2003. http://seattlepi.nwsource.com/local/104115_suicide15.shtml.
2. Quoted in Katherine Ramsland, "Andrea Yates: Ill or Evil?," Crime Library, 2007. www.crimelibrary.com/notorious_murders/women/andrea_yates/index.html.

Chapter 1: What Is Postpartum Depression?

3. Brooke Shields, *Down Came the Rain: My Journey Through Postpartum Depression*, New York: Hyperion, 2005, p. 79.
4. Shoshana S. Bennett and Pec Indman, "Beyond the Blues: A Guide to Understanding and Treating Prenatal Postpartum Depression," Moodswings, 2003. www.postpartum.net/brief.html.
5. Shaila Kulkarni Misri, *Pregnancy Blues: What Every Woman Needs to Know About Depression During Pregnancy*, New York: Delacorte, 2005, p. 113.
6. Jeff Minerd, U.S. Psych: Postpartum Depression and Psychosis Easily Missed," *Psychiatric Times*, November 21, 2006.
7. Dean Rafflock, "Postpartum Depression (PPD)," Pregnancy Recovery, undated. www.pregnancyrecovery.com/postpartumdepression.cfm.
8. Misri, *Pregnancy Blues: What Every Woman Needs to Know About Depression During Pregnancy*, p. 130.

Chapter 2: Diagnosis and Drug Treatment

9. Misri, *Pregnancy Blues: What Every Woman Needs to Know About Depression During Pregnancy*, p. 12.

Notes

10. C. Neill Epperson, "Postpartum Major Depression: Detection and Treatment," *American Family Physician*, April 15, 1999. www.aafp.org/afp/990415ap/2247.htm.
11. Ronald Rosenberg, Deborah Greening, and James Windell, *Conquering Postpartum Depression: A Proven Plan for Recovery*, Cambridge, MA: Perseus, 2003, p. 94.
12. Misri, *Pregnancy Blues: What Every Woman Needs to Know About Depression During Pregnancy*, p. 186.
13. Misri, *Pregnancy Blues: What Every Woman Needs to Know About Depression During Pregnancy*, p. 188.
14. Sandra L. Wheatley, *Coping With Postnatal Depression*, London: Sheldon Press, 2005, p. 28.

Chapter 3: Nondrug Therapies

15. Rosenberg, Greening, and Windell, *Conquering Postpartum Depression: A Proven Plan for Recovery*, p. 94.
16. Misri, *Pregnancy Blues: What Every Woman Needs to Know About Depression During Pregnancy*, p. 204.
17. Misri, *Pregnancy Blues: What Every Woman Needs to Know About Depression During Pregnancy*, p. 215.
18. Rosenberg, Greening, and Windell, *Conquering Postpartum Depression: A Proven Plan for Recovery*, p. 137-138.
19. Dean Raffelock, "Allopathic and Natural Treatments for Postpartum Depression...Which is Best for You?," Pregnancy Recovery, undated. www.pregnancyrecovery.com/library/allopathic.cfm.
20. Misri, *Pregnancy Blues: What Every Woman Needs to Know About Depression During Pregnancy*, p. 219.
21. Victoria Hendrick, "Alternative Treatments for Postpartum Depression," *Psychiatric Times*, August 2003, Vol. XX, Iss. 8. www.psychiatrictimes.com/Depressive-Disorders/Postpartum-Depression/showArticle.jhtml;jsessionid=2SURXZWMLWP3IQSNDLPSKHSCJUNN2JVN?checkSite=psychiatricTimes&articleID=175802525.

Chapter 4: Effects of PPD on the Child and Others

22. Misri, *Pregnancy Blues: What Every Woman Needs to Know About Depression During Pregnancy*, p. 190.

23. Quoted in HealthyPlace.com, "Antidepressants and Breastfeeding," July 6, 2001. http://72.14.253.104/search?q=cache:6kXc8POmklkJ:www.healthyplace.com/Communities/depression/treatment/antidepressants/breastfeeding.asp+antidepressants+and+breast+feeding&hl=en&ct=clnk&cd=1&gl=us.
24. Ruth A. Lawrence, "Herbs and Breastfeeding," Breastfeeding.com, 2007. www.breastfeeding.com/reading_room/herbs.html.
25. Margaret L. Moline, David A. Kahn, Ruth W. Ross, Lori L. Altshuler, and Lee S. Cohen, "Postpartum Depression: A Guide for Patients and Families, Psychguides.com, March 2001. http://72.14.253.104/search?q=cache:PxUa1PJKJAoJ:www.psychguides.com/DinW%2520postpartum.pdf+postpartum+depression+untreated+effect+on+the+child&hl=en&ct=clnk&cd=3&gl=us.
26. Misri, *Pregnancy Blues: What Every Woman Needs to Know About Depression During Pregnancy*, p. 242.
27. Quoted in WebMD, "Study: Dads Get Postpartum Depression: Research Says 14% Of Mothers, 10% Of Fathers Suffer Symptoms," Aug. 7, 2006. www.netscape.com/viewstory/2006/08/07/dads-get-postpartum-depression-research-says-14-percent-of-mothers-10-percent-of-fathers-suffer-symp/?url=http%3A%2F%2Fwww.cbsnews.com%2Fstories%2F2006%2F08%2F07%2Fhealth%2Fwebmd%2Fmain1870726.shtml%3Fsource%3DRSS%26attr%3DHOME_1870726&frame=true.
28. Quoted in Daniel DeNoon, "Dads Have Postpartum Depression, Too: Depression in Father Doubles Risk of Child's Later Behavior Problems," *WebMD Medical News*, June 23, 2005. www.webmd.com/content/article/107/108672.htm.
29. Quoted in Ed Edelson, "Postpartum Depression Hits Dads, Too: Study Finds 10 Percent of New Fathers Struggle With the Condition," *ScoutNews*, August 7, 2006. www.healthcentral.com/depression/news-534203-105.html.
30. Quoted in DeNoon, "Dads Have Postpartum Depression, Too: Depression in Father Doubles Risk of Child's Later Behavior Problems."

Notes

Chapter 5: The Road to Recovery

31. Rosenberg, Greening, and Windell, *Conquering Postpartum Depression: A Proven Plan for Recovery*, p. 74.
32. Quoted in Cbsnews.com, "What's Up With Tom Cruise?," June 6, 2005. www.cbsnews.com/stories/2005/06/06/early-show/leisure/celebspot/main699852.shtml.
33. Quoted in Rosenberg, Greening, and Windell, *Conquering Postpartum Depression: A Proven Plan for Recovery*, p. 77.
34. Sandra L. Wheatley, *Coping With Postnatal Depression*, p. 41.
35. Rosenberg, Greening, and Windell, *Conquering Postpartum Depression: A Proven Plan for Recovery*, pp. 141-142.
36. Sandra L. Wheatley, *Coping With Postnatal Depression*, pp. 59-60.
37. Quoted in Linda Harbrecht, "Helping Others Combat Postpartum Depression," Lehigh University, February 3, 2006. www3.lehigh.edu/News/news_story.asp?iNewsID=1625.
38. Quoted in Harbrecht, "Helping Others Combat Postpartum Depression," Lehigh University.
39. Marie Osmond, Marcia Wilkie, and Judith Moore, *Behind the Smile*: *My Journey Out of Postpartum Depression*, New York: Warner Books, 2001, p. 288.

Glossary

acetylcholine: A type of neurotransmitter related to pleasure and relaxation that helps regulate mood.

acupuncture: A traditional Chinese medical practice that works by inserting tiny needles at particular points in the body believed to be meridians for "chi," a Chinese word meaning life energy.

agoraphobia: Extreme fear and anxiety only in certain places or situations, such as airplanes, bridges, tunnels, and elevators.

alternative medicine: A broad term that refers to a variety of unconventional treatments that are seen as alternatives to the various drugs offered by doctors trained in Western medicine.

anemia: A condition in which the body is deprived of oxygen needed to function properly and which can be the result of a diet low in B vitamins or iron.

anorexia: An eating disorder characterized by a lack of appetite or a total aversion to food.

anticonvulsants: A class of medications used for treating depression.

antidepressant: A class of medications used to treat symptoms of depression.

anxiety disorder: A mental illness that produces an intense and excessive state of apprehension and fear.

aromatherapy: An alternative treatment that uses essential oils and plant essences to stimulate the immune system and encourage healing.

Glossary

atypical antipsychotics: A class of medications used for treating depression.

baby blues: A temporary period of mild depression experienced by many women after childbirth that usually dissipates without treatment.

benzodiazepines: A class of medications used for treating anxiety.

bipolar disorder: A mental illness in which patients experience wild mood swings that range from deep despair to extreme happiness, or mania, when they have increased energy and zest for life.

bulimia: An eating disorder characterized by eating too much (bingeing) and then throwing up (purging).

cognitive behavior therapy (CBT): A psychotherapy technique that combines cognitive therapy, which helps to change thinking patterns, with behavioral therapy, which focuses on changing behavior that may be contributing to depression.

cortisol: A natural hormone used by the body to fight stress and inflammation.

Couvade syndrome: A psychiatric tendency in which fathers sympathize with their pregnant wives, sometimes developing physical symptoms of pregnancy.

Diagnostic and Statistical Manual of Mental Disorders (DSM-IV): A manual published by the American Psychiatric Association that lists mental health disorders.

dopamine: A type of brain neurotransmitter related to pleasure and relaxation that helps regulate mood.

Edinburgh Postnatal Depression Scale (EPDS): A questionnaire developed by doctors in the United Kingdom to help primary care physicians detect PPD.

electroconvulsive therapy (ECT): The use of electric current to alter the electro-chemical processes in the brain.

family therapy: A type of psychotherapy that focuses on family or couples' relationship problems.

5-Hydroxytryptophan (5-HTP): A by-product of tryptophan, an amino acid necessary for the body's production of serotonin.

gamma-aminobutyric acid (GABA): A type of brain neurotransmitter related to pleasure and relaxation that helps regulate mood.

group therapy: A type of psychotherapy in which six or more people meet as a group to share their problems and experiences.

hallucination: A symptom of mental illness in which the patient sees, hears, or otherwise senses things that are not real.

homeopathy: A system of medicine designed to stimulate the body's own natural defense mechanisms by treating patients with greatly diluted solutions of plant extracts.

hormones: A naturally occurring chemical substance used to initiate, control, or regulate physical changes in various parts of the body.

hypothyroidism: A condition caused by the thyroid gland's insufficient production of the hormone thyroxin and by a lack of iodine.

insulin: A hormone produced by the body to convert sugar, starch, and other foods into energy.

interpersonal psychotherapy (IPT): A psychotherapy treatment that seeks to improve the patient's self-esteem and communication skills with family members and friends.

light therapy: An alternative treatment that uses bright light to lift depression.

lithium: A mood stabilizing medication.

Glossary

massage: An alternative treatment that manipulates the soft tissues of the body to increase relaxation.

metoclopramide: A medication, sold under the brand name Reglan, often prescribed to women to help control the nausea and vomiting that are common during pregnancy.

Monoamine Oxidase Inhibitors (MAOIs): A type of antidepressant medication that works by affecting serotonin and norepinephrine, but which are often avoided in postpartum cases due to significant side effects.

mood stabilizers: A class of medication used for treating bipolar disorders.

neurotransmitters: Naturally occurring chemicals in the human brain that transmit nerve impulses from one brain cell to another.

norepinephrine: A type of hormone and neurotransmitter used by the body to respond to stress with a "fight-or-flight" response that causes the heart to beat faster and the lungs to breathe more deeply.

obsessive-compulsive disorder (OCD): A type of anxiety disorder characterized by persistent, obsessive thoughts and repetitive, compulsive behaviors.

panic attack: An intense and sudden feeling of fear and anxiety, often accompanied by physical symptoms such as heart palpitations, shortness of breath, sweating, trembling, rapid breathing, nausea, dizziness, or feeling faint.

postpartum: The period following pregnancy and childbirth.

postpartum depression (PPD): A mental illness that occurs during the period after the birth of a child.

psychiatrist: A physician who specializes in the prevention, diagnosis, and treatment of mental illness. Psychiatrists can prescribe medicine to their patients.

psychodynamic psychotherapy: A type of psychotherapy that focuses on identifying negative patterns from a patient's past that may be responsible for present day problems.

psychologist: A professional that specializes in diagnosing and treating mental illness. Psychologists are PhDs but they cannot prescribe medication to their patients.

psychostimulants: A class of medication used for treating depression and known to boost energy and decrease sleepiness, lethargy, and fatigue.

psychotherapy: The treatment of mental and emotional disorders using psychological methods, such as counseling.

psychotic or psychosis: A type of severe mental illness characterized by loss of contact with reality and symptoms such as hallucinations, delusions, withdrawal, and sometimes suicidal or homicidal thoughts.

reflexology: An alternative treatment that involves massaging reflex points on the hands or feet to stimulate the nervous system.

Selective Serotonin Reuptake Inhibitors (SSRIs): A widely used antidepressant medication that works by increasing levels of serotonin.

serotonin: A type of neurotransmitter that helps regulate mood.

Serotonin Norepinephrine Reuptake Inhibitors (SNRIs): A type of antidepressant medication that affects norepinephrine neurotransmitters and has been effective in achieving complete remission of depression symptoms in postpartum women.

St. John's Wort (hypericum perforatum): An herb used to treat depression.

thyroid gland: A gland that controls the body's metabolism rate and immune system.

Glossary

Trycyclics (TCAs): A type of antidepressant medication that affects serotonin and norepinephrine, but has significant side effects. TCAs are infrequently used in postpartum cases.

tryptophan: An amino acid that the human body uses to make serotonin.

Organizations to Contact

American College of Obstetricians and Gynecologists (ACOG)
209 12th St., S.W., Washington, D.C. 20090-6920
Ph: (202) 484-3321
Web site: www.acog.com

The American College of Obstetricians and Gynecologists (ACOG) is the nation's leading group of professionals providing health care for women. A search of this Web site produces a list of publications on postpartum depression.

Mother-to-Mother Postpartum Depression Network
A New Day, Inc., P.O. Box 797381, Dallas, TX 75379
Ph: (214) 549-5318
Email: Sandra.Poulin@postpartumdepression.net
Web site: www.postpartumdepression.net/

This is a Web site for a book about postpartum depression that contains real life stories of women who have successfully battled the disease.

National Association of Mothers' Centers (NAMC)
64 Division Ave., Levittown, NY 11756
Ph: (516) 520-2929
Fax: (516)520-1639
Email: info@motherscenter.org
Web site: www.motherscenter.org

The National Association of Mothers' Centers (NAMC) is a national organization that promotes and coordinates local, non-profit mothers' centers where women can meet and engage in discussion groups to help them with their roles as mothers. The Web site lists mothers' centers in various states and contains a useful resource list of organizations of interest to mothers.

Postpartum Support International (PSI)

927 N. Kellogg Ave., Santa Barbara, CA 93111
Ph: (805) 967-7636
Fax: (805) 967-0608
Email: PSIOffice@earthlink.net
Web site: www.postpartum.net

Postpartum Support International (PSI) is a support group founded in 1987 by Jane Honikman in Santa Barbara, California. It seeks to increase awareness among public and professional communities about the emotional changes that women experience during pregnancy and the postpartum period. PSI's Web site lists a telephone help number as well as contact information for support groups around the United States.

The Postpartum Stress Center

1062 Lancaster Ave., Rosemont Plaza, Ste. 2, Rosemont, PA 19010
Ph: (610) 525-7527
Fax: (610) 525-3997
Email: kkleiman@aol.com
Web site: www.postpartumstress.com/

The Postpartum Stress Center was founded in 1988 by Karen Kleiman, a psychotherapist, to provide a better understanding and comprehensive clinical intervention for any woman who suffers from the range of postpartum psychiatric disorders. The Web site provides valuable information about the symptoms and treatments of postpartum depression and provides evaluations and phone consultations for women who may be suffering from the illness.

For More Information

Books

Sandra Poulin Berkley, *The Mother-to-Mother Postpartum Depression Support Book: Real Stories from Women Who Lived Through It and Recovered*, Berkeley, CA: Berkeley Trade Paperback, 2006. A collection of stories about ordinary women who suffered from postpartum depression.

Arlene Huysman and Paul J. Goodnick, *The Postpartum Effect: Deadly Depression in Mothers*, New York: Seven Stories Press, 2003. An instructive book by a clinical psychologist about postpartum depression, with a focus on cases that resulted in child homicide.

Pec Indman and Shoshana S. Bennett, *Beyond the Blues*, San Jose, CA: Moodswings Press, 2003. An informative manual on postpartum depression.

Natasha S. Mauthner, *The Darkest Days of My Life*, Boston, MA: Harvard University Press, 2002. Interviews with thirty-five new mothers in Britain and the United States discussing their struggle with postpartum depression.

Dr. Dean Raffelock, *A Natural Guide to Pregnancy and Postpartum Health*, New York: Avery, 2002. A book about how to prevent and remedy postpartum problems through natural methods such as diet, exercise, hormone-balancing, the use of medicinal herbs and nutritional supplements, as well as the use of conventional medications.

Susan Kushner Resnick, *Sleepless Days: One Woman's Journey Through Postpartum Depression*, New York: St. Martin's Press, 2000. One woman's poignant memoir about her depression and recovery from postpartum depression.

Tina Zahn and Wanda Dyson, *Why I Jumped: My True Story of Postpartum Depression, Dramatic Rescue & Return to Hope*, Grand Rapids, MI: Fleming H. Revell, 2006. The story of Tina Zahn, a woman suffering from postpartum depression, who tried to leap from a bridge but was caught by a police officer.

Periodicals and Newspapers

Marianne McGinnism "Baby blues? Get Help Early," *Prevention*, January 2006, Vol. 58, Iss. 1, p. 107.

Carl Sherman, "Mild Postpartum Depression: Try Nondrug Options," *Family Practice News*, June 1, 2005, Vol. 35, Iss. 11, p. 42.

Katherine Stone, "My Turn: Why I Was Scared That I Might Hurt My Baby," *Newsweek*, June 7, 2006. www.msnbc.msn.com/id/5085224/site/newsweek/.

Michele G. Sullivan, "Fathers Can Get Postpartum Depression, Too," *Clinical Psychiatry News*, May 2006, Vol. 34, Iss. 5, p. 27.

Laurie Tarkan, "Dealing With Depression and the Perils of Pregnancy," *New York Times*, January 13, 2004.

Molly Triffin, "The Truth About Baby Blues: More Women Are Admitting They Hit a Low After Having a Kid. Cosmo Shines a Light on Their Secret Suffering," *Cosmopolitan*, December 2005, Vol. 239, Iss. 6, p. 152.

USA Today Magazine, "Depressed Women Should Seek Treatment," February 2004, Vol. 132, Iss. 2705, p. 2.

Geoff Williams, "My Superstar Wife: Battling Her Postpartum Depression Makes My Better Half a Bigger Action Hero Than Tom Cruise Could Ever Be," *Baby Talk*, September 1, 2005, Vol. 70, Iss. 7, p. 83.

Web Sites

Online Postpartum Depression Support Group (www.ppdsupportpage.com). An online support group for women suffering from postpartum depression.

Postpartum Dads (www.postpartumdads.org). A volunteer-based outreach project affiliated with Postpartum Support International (www.postpartum.net) that focuses on providing support for fathers.

Postpartum Progress (http://postpartumprogress.typepad.com/weblog/2005/11/ppd_support_gro.html). A blog site with many useful links to information and resources on postpartum depression.

WellMother.com (www.wellmother.com). An online resource for women and their families designed to offer support and resources on a number of issues relating to women's health, including postpartum depression.

Women's Mental Health Program at Emory University (www.emorywomensprogram.org). A university Web site that focuses on the evaluation and treatment of mental disorders during pregnancy and the postpartum period.

Index

A Beautiful Mind (movie), 42
Acetylcholine, 25
Acquired immune deficiency syndrome (AIDS), 7, 37
Acupuncture/alternative therapies, 46, 49–50, 53–57
Advice, for fathers, 78
Agoraphobia, 17
Alprazolam (Xanax), 41
Ambien (zolpidem), 41
American Academy of Pediatrics, 61, 69
American Psychiatric Association, 17
Anemia, 28, 37
Anorexia, 22, 23
Anticonvulsant medications, 40
Antidepressant medications, 39–40, 46, 62, 73
Antipsychotic medications, 40, 63
Anxiety, 14, 23
Appetite problems, 15

Beck, C. T., 82
Behind the Smile: My Journey Out of Postpartum Depression (Osmond), 35
Benzodiazepines, 40, 41, 63
Bingeing, 22
Bipolar disorder (manic-depressive illness)
  description/dangers of, 23
  drug treatments for, 41–43
Birth control pills, 50
Breast-feeding, 61–64
Bright light therapy, 47, 54, 64
Bulimia, 22, 23

Calcium supplements, 52

Carbamazepine (Tegretol), 63
Celebrities, with PPD
  Cox, Courtney, 35
  Osmond, Marie, 35, 83
  Shields, Brooke, 16–17, 35, 73
  Spears, Britney, 35
Celexa (citalopram), 40, 62
Center for Pediatric Research, 68
Childbirth
  causes of depression after, 37
  mental disorders triggered by, 22
  PPD triggered by, 14
Children
  effects of alternate treatments on, 64–65
  effects of mother's medication on, 61–64
  effects of non-treatment on, 65–66
Citalopram (Celexa), 40, 62
Clonazepam (Klonopin), 41
Cognitive behavior therapy (CBT), 46
Coleman, William, 69
Copper insufficiency, 29
Cortisol (stress hormone), 26
Couples therapy, 48–49
Couvade syndrome, 66
Cox, Courtney, 35
Cruise, Tom, 73
Crying, 14
Cymbalta (duloxetine), 40

Delusions, 23, 42
Depakote (valproic acid), 63
Depression
  foods helpful for, 53

neurotransmitters linked with, 25
of new mothers, 15
nutritional supplements for, 51
possible causes of, 37
slow symptom development, 31–32
St. John's wort for, 49–50
women and, 19
Despair, 15, 23
Diabetes, 37
Diagnosis, of PPD
　EPDS questionnaire for, 32–34, 36
　interview of patient, 37–38
　medical assessment, 36–37
　obstacles to, 30–32
　psychiatric history consideration, 29
　See also Edinburgh Postnatal Depression Scale
Diagnostic and Statistical Manual of Mental Disorders (DSM-IV), 17
Diazepam (Valium), 41
DiMatteo, Robin, 74
Dopamine, 25
Down Came the Rain: My Journey Through Postpartum Depression (Shields), 16–17, 35
Drug combinations, for PPD, 40–41
Duloxetine (Cymbalta), 40

Eating disorders, 22, 23, 29, 49
Eating patterns, 37
Edinburgh Postnatal Depression Scale (EPDS), 32–34, 36
Effexor (venlafaxine), 40, 62

Elation, 23
Electroconvulsive therapy (ECT), 42, 43
Endorphins, 54
Eosinophilic myalgia syndrome (EMS), 53
EPDS. *See* Edinburgh Postnatal Depression Scale (EPDS)
Epperson, C. Neill, 32
Essential oils/plant essences, 57
Estrogen, 25, 26

Family therapy, 45, 48–49
Fathers
　advice for, 78
　postpartum depression and, 66–69
Fears, unexplained, 17
Federline, Kevin, 35
Fight-or-flight response, 25
5-hydroxytryptophan (5-HTP), 53
Fluoxetine (Prozac), 36, 40
Folic acid deficiency, 28

Gabapentin (Neurontin), 63
Gamma-aminobutyric acid (GABA), 25
Genetics, role of, 20
Greening, Deborah, 39, 44, 50, 77
Group therapy, 45, 47–48

Hallucinations, 23
Heart palpitations, 17
Hendrick, Victoria, 57
Hepatitis, 37
Herbal supplements, 46, 49–50
Homeopathic medicine, 55
Homicidal thoughts, 23
Hopelessness, 16
Hormonal fluctuations, 14, 25,

Index

28, 49
Hormonal patches, 41
Hypericum perforatum (St. John's Word herb), 49–50, 64–65
Hypnosis, 57

Infectious diseases, 37
Interpersonal psychotherapy (IPT), 46
Interview of patient, for PPD, 37–38
Iodine deficiency, 28
Iron deficiency, 28
Irritability, 14
Isolation, 17

Klonopin (clonazepam), 41

Lamictal (lamotrigine), 63
Lamotrigine (Lamictal), 63
Lawrence, Ruth A., 64
Lithium, 41–42, 62–63
Lusskin, Shari L., 69

Magnesium supplements, 52
Manic-depressive illness. *See* Bipolar disorder (manic-depressive illness)
Massage, 55, 57, 64
Mayo Clinic medical facility, 20
Medical assessment, for PPD, 36–37
Medications, for PPD
  antidepressant medications, 39–40
  bipolar/psychotic drug treatments, 41–43
  drug combinations, 40–41
  effects on breast-fed infants, 61–64
Melatonin, 54
Metoclopramide (Reglan), 37

Misri, Shaila Kulkarni, 20, 29, 42, 45, 48, 55, 61, 68
Monoamine oxidase inhibitors (MAOIs), 39
Mononucleosis, 37
Mood disorders, 14
Mood stabilizer medications, 40, 63
Moore, Judith, 52, 83

Neglect of baby, by parents, 69
Neurontin (gabapentin), 63
Neurotransmitters
  depression linked with, 24–25
  norepinephrine neurotransmitters, 25, 40
  nutritional precursors for, 50
  pregnancy's influence on, 26
Nondrug therapies, 44–59
  acupuncture/alternative therapies, 53–57
  herbal supplements, 49–50
  nutritional supplements, 50–53
  psychotherapy treatment, 44–49
  self-help strategies, 57–59
Non-treatment of PPD, effects on child, 65–66
Nutrition
  nutritional supplements, 50–53
  underlying deficiencies of, 28–29

Obsessive-compulsive disorder (OCD), 18, 21
Olanzapine (Zyprexa), 40
Omega-3/Omega-6 fatty acids, 52, 53
One Flew Over the Cuckoo's

Nest (movie), 42
Osmond, Marie, 35, 83
Osteopathic medicine, 52

Panic anxiety disorder, 17–18
Parenting classes, 49
Paroxetine (Paxil), 40
Paxil (paroxetine), 40, 62, 63
Plant essences, 57
Postpartum depression (PPD)
  behaviors of women with, 22–23
  biological causes of, 24–26
  fathers and, 66–69
  levels of, 14–17
  nondrug therapies for, 44–59
  psychological risk factors of, 26–28
  road to recovery from, 72–83
  role of nutrition in, 28–29
  symptoms of, 14–16
  triggers of, 14, 28
  United Kingdom study of, 26
  variations of, 17–23
  vitamins for, 52
Postpartum Progress Web site, 79
Postpartum psychosis, 23–24
Postpartum Support International support group, 18
Post-traumatic stress disorder (PTSD), 21
development by new mothers, 22
PPD. *See* Postpartum depression (PPD)
Pregnancy
  control of nausea/vomiting during, 37
  mental disorders triggered by, 22
  neurotransmitter changes during, 26
  vulnerability to anemia during, 37
Progesterone, 25, 26
Prozac (fluoxetine), 36, 40, 62
Psychodynamic psychotherapy, 46–47
Psychological risk factors, of PPD, 26–28
Psychostimulant medications, 40, 41
Psychotherapy treatment, 38, 44–49
  cognitive behavior therapy, 46
  couples/family therapy, 48–49
  group therapy, 48
  interpersonal psychotherapy, 46
  parenting classes, 49
  psychodynamic psychotherapy, 46–47
Psychotic drug treatments, 41–43

Quetiapine (Seroquel), 40–41

Raffelock, Dean, 28, 50
Ramchandani, Paul, 70
Recovery, from postpartum depression
  adopting positive behaviors, 75–78
  becoming confident parent, 79–80
  following treatment plan, 72–74
  signs of, 81–82
  slow recovery, 80–81
  support during, 79–80
  working with doctors during, 74–75
Reglan (metoclopramide), 37
Resnick, Phillip J., 24

Index

Risperdal (risperidone), 41
Risperidone (Risperdal), 41
Rosenberg, Ronald, 39, 44, 50, 77
Rosenberg, Tonya, battle with PPD, 36

Sadness, 14, 15
Screening tools, for PPD
  Edinburgh Postnatal Depression Scale, 32–34, 36
  interview of patient, 37
Seasonal Affective Disorder (SAD), 47
Selective norepinephrine reuptake inhibitors (SNRIs), 39, 40
Selective serotonin reuptake inhibitors (SSRIs), 39, 51
Self-help strategies, 57–59
Self-nurturing, 59
Seroquel (quetiapine), 40–41
Serotonin, 25, 26, 40
Sertraline (Zoloft), 40, 62, 63
Shields, Brooke, 16–17, 35, 73
Sleeping difficulties, 14
Social pressure/problems, linked with PPD, 27, 32
Spears, Britney, 35
Spiritual rituals, 59
Stone, Katherine, 79
Stowe, Zachary, 61
Stress hormone (cortisol), 26
Sudden infant death syndrome (SIDS), 20
Suicidal thoughts, 16, 23

Talk therapy. *See* Psychotherapy treatment
Tegretol (carbamazepine), 63
Testosterone, 25–26
Thyroid disorders, 28, 37
Thyroxine insufficiency, 28
Topamax (topiramate), 63

Topiramate (Topamax), 63
Transcendental Meditation program, 59
Treatment plan, for PPD
  antidepressant medications, 39–40
  bipolar/psychotic medications, 41–43
  drug combinations, 40–41
  electroconvulsive therapy, 42, 43
  psychotherapy, 38, 44–49
Trembling, 17
Tricyclics (TCAs), 39
Triggers, of postpartum depression, 28
Tryptophan, 25, 53

United Kingdom, postpartum depression study, 26

Valium (diazepam), 41
Venlafaxine (Effexor), 40
Vitamin B complex, 52
Vitamin B6, 53
Vitamin B12, 53
Vitamin B-12 deficiency, 28

Wheatley, Sandra L., 43, 77
Windell, James, 39, 44, 50, 77
Women
  behaviors of women with, 22–23
  depression and, 19
World Health Organization, 61

Xanax (alprazolam), 41

Yale University School of Medicine, 32
Yoga, 59

Zoloft (sertraline), 40, 62, 63
Zolpidem (Ambien), 41
Zyprexa (olanzapine), 40

Picture Credits

Cover: Courtesy of photos.com
© Ajax/zefa/Corbis, 62
AP Images, 83
© Atlantide Phototravel/Corbis, 45
© Axel Koester/Corbis, 16
© Bohemian Nomad Picturemakers/Corbis, 45
© Brenda Ann Kenneally/Corbis, 27
© Corbis SYGMA, 10
Colin Anderson/ Brand X Pictures/Jupiter Images, 56
© Dana Hoff/Beateworks/Corbis, 58
© Ed Quinn/Corbis, 22
Handout/Getty Images News/Getty Images, 12, 13
Image Source Pink/Jupiter Images, 56
Imagemore/ Creatas Images/Jupiter Images, 58
Jose Luis Pelaez/Getty Images, 31
© Jutta Klee/Corbis, 56
Karen Kasmauski/Getty Images, 48
© Katy Winn/Corbis, 35
© Ken Seet/Corbis, 55
© Louie Psihoyos/Corbis, 54
© Mark Savage/Corbis, 35
© Michael Macor/San Francisco Chronicle/Corbis, 21
© Mika/zefa/Corbis, 24
© Pat Doyle/Corbis, 18
© Reuters/Corbis, 9
© Solus-Veer/Corbis, 60
Todd Meier/Glasshouse Images/Jupiter Images, 15
© Visuals Unlimited/Corbis, 38, 51
© Will & Deni McIntyre/Corbis, 76

About the Author

Debra A. Miller is a writer and lawyer with a passion for current events and history. She began her law career in Washington, DC, where she worked on legislative, policy, and legal matters in government, public interest, and private law firm positions. She now lives with her husband in Encinitas, California. She has written and edited numerous books and anthologies on historical, political, health, and other topics.